7/21/21

"Nostalgic Blood"

by

J. Crockett

Full Definition of NOSTALGIA

1
: the state of being homesick : homesickness
2
: a wistful or excessively sentimental yearning for return
to or of some past period or irrecoverable condition; ALSO
: something that evokes nostalgia

nostalgic

adjective sentimental, longing, emotional, homesick,
wistful, maudlin, regretful I got nostalgic the other night
and dug out my old photos.

Blood in this novel represent
familyBloodline definitionYour *bloodline*
is your heritage or ancestry. In other
words, your *bloodline* includes your
parents, grandparents, great-
grandparents, and so on.

The Old English root word *blod*, means
"blood." By the 13th century, *blood* also
meant "family" or "heritage."

Market Monster Publishing, LLC.
Email: marketmonsterpublishing@gmail.com

Ordering Information:
Quantity sales. Special discounts are available on quantity purchases by corporations, associations, and others. For details, contact the publisher at the address above.
Orders by U.S. trade bookstores and wholesalers. Please contact Big Distribution: Tel: 773-563-3947

Acknowledgements

- No one walks alone on the journey of life. Just where do you start to thank those that joined you, walked beside you, and helped you along the way continuously urged me to write a book, to put my thoughts down on over the years, those that I have met and worked with have paper, and to share my insights together with the secrets to my continual, positive approach to life and all that life throws at us. So at last, here it is. So, perhaps this book and its pages will be seen as "thanks" to the tens of thousands of you who have helped make my life what is today. Much of what I have learned over the years will be identified as you read this book. Some of your names had to be changed, but I am sure that you guys would understand. Many of you have inspired me and, subconsciously contributed a tremendous amount to the content of this book. A little bit of each of them will be found here weaving in and out of the pages – in loving memory for those who did not make it out alive. I also have to thank Roseanne Beam for being supportive, motivating and pushed me beyond description, which I can't say. I also need to thank my mom Annie Copeland, wonderful woman who kept me under her wing; any time my mind strayed I thought about how she would feel. My step dad Andy Copeland for being a guide in my life. My dad, Joseph Crockett thank you for being so honest about life in general. You saved me in many ways. Even though you don't think my book will do well, time will tell.

- It's strange to think that I have been working on this book for 20 years. I lost it three times, recovered it somehow through the grace of the higher power; I believe it was meant for me to complete this book and share my story with the world. Valencia Copeland, I can't thank you enough for everything you have done. Vivian Copeland, keep inventing because it's worth it. I also want to thank all of you who took the time out of your day to help with the book cover survey, thanks guys. That helped me.

- I want to thank Custom Plastic and signs, Chris Cuevas for being so patient with me with designing the book cover. I know I can be picky, if not for your expertise, who knows what the book cover would look like. For any printing of signs, plastic moldings, Chris can do it. Call him 209 933 9711

- Lyrell McGee, thanks for everything you did, just did not have enough time, when you ready to publish, I will be there for you.

- Last but not least, I want to thank all of the Stocktonians who took a chance and bought my book. Some of you gave me whatever you had as a donation to help me climb to the level of publishing. It was you, the residents of Stockton, Ca that helped me get into the stores worldwide. Thank you so much. Look forwarded to more great books from me.

North Korea (listen), officially the**Democratic People's Republic of Korea**(**DPRK**; Chosŏn'gŭl: 조선민주주의인민공화국;hancha: 朝鮮民主主義人民共和國;MR: *Chosŏn Minjujuŭi Inmin Konghwaguk*), is a country in East Asia, in the northern part of the Korean Peninsula. The name *Korea* is derived from the Kingdom of Goryeo, also spelled as *Koryŏ*. The capital and largest city is Pyongyang. North Korea shares a land border with China to the north and north-west, along the Amnok (Yalu) and Tumen rivers, and a small section of the Tumen River also forms a border with Russia to the north-east.[8] The Korean Demilitarized Zone marks the *de facto* boundary between North Korea and South Korea. The legitimacy of this border is not accepted by either side, as both states claim to be the legitimate government of the entire peninsula.

The Empire of Japan annexed Korea in 1910. After the Japanese surrender at the end ofWorld War II in 1945, Korea was divided into two zones by the United States and the Soviet Union, with the north occupied by the Sovietsand the south by the Americans. Negotiations on reunification failed, and in 1948 two separate governments were formed: the Democratic People's Republic of Korea in the north, and the Republic of Korea in the south. These conflicting claims of sovereignty led to the Korean War (1950–53). Although theKorean Armistice Agreement brought about a ceasefire, no official peace treaty was ever signed.[9] Both states were accepted into theUnited Nations in 1991.[10]

The DPRK officially describes itself as a self-reliant socialist state and holds elections.[11]Internationally, however, it is considered atotalitarian dictatorship. Various outlets have called it Stalinist,[20][21][22] particularly noting the elaborate cult of personality around Kim Il-sung and his family. International organizations have also assessed human rights violations in North Korea as belonging to a category of their own, with no parallel in the contemporary world.[23][24][25] TheWorkers' Party of Korea, led by a member of the ruling family,[22] holds power in the state and leads the Democratic Front for the Reunification of the Fatherland of which all political officers are required to be a member.[26]

Over time North Korea has gradually distanced itself from the world communistmovement. *Juche*, an ideology of national self-reliance, was introduced into the constitution as a "creative application ofMarxism–Leninism" in 1972.[27][28] Themeans of production are owned by the state through state-run enterprises andcollectivized farms. Most services such as healthcare, education, housing and food production are subsidized or state-funded.[29]In the late 1990s, North Korea suffered from a famine that resulted in the deaths of hundreds of thousands of civilians; the country continues to struggle with food production.[30]

North Korea follows *Songun*, or "military-first" policy.[31] It is the world's most militarizedsociety, with a total of 9,495,000 active,reserve, and paramilitarypersonnel[*citation needed*]. Its active duty army of 1.21 million is the fourth largest in the world, after China, the U.S., and India.[32] It also possesses nuclear weapons.[33][34]

Nostalgic Blood takes place during the Kim Jong Il dictatorship, from biography.com is his life story.

Kim Jong Il's dominating personality and complete concentration of power has come to define the country North Korea. Born in either 1941 or 1942, much of Kim Jong Il's persona is based on a cult of personality, meaning that legend and official North Korean government accounts describe his life, character, and actions in ways that promote and legitimize his leadership, including his birth. Over the years, Kim's dominating personality and complete concentration of power has come to define the country North Korea.

Early Life

Born February 16, 1941, though official accounts place birth a year later. Some mystery surrounds when and where Kim Jong Il was born. Official North Korean biographies state that his birth occurred on February 16, 1942, in a secret camp on Mount Paekdu along the Chinese border, in Samjiyon County, Ryanggang Province, in the Democratic People's Republic of Korea (North Korea). Other reports indicate he was born a year later in Vyatskoye in the former Soviet Union.

During World War II, his father commanded the 1st Battalion of the Soviet 88th Brigade, composed of Chinese and Korean exiles battling the Japanese Army. Kim Jong Il's mother was Kim Jong Suk, his father's first wife. Official accounts indicate that Kim Jong Il comes from a family of nationalists who actively resisted imperialism from the Japanese in the early 20th century.

His official government biography claims Kim Jong Il completed his general education between September 1950 and August 1960 in Pyongyang, the current capital city of North Korea. But scholars point out that the first few years of this period were during the Korean War and contend his early education took place in the People's Republic of China, where it was safer to live. Official accounts claim that throughout his schooling, Kim was involved in politics. While attending the Namsan Higher Middle School in Pyongyang, he was active in the Children's Union—a youth organization that promotes the concept of Juche, or the spirit of self-reliance—and the Democratic Youth League (DYL), taking part in the study of Marxist political theory. During his youth, Kim Jong Il showed an interest in a wide range of subjects including agriculture, music, and mechanics. In high school, he took classes in automotive repair and participated in trips to farms and factories. Official accounts of his early schooling also point out his leadership capabilities: as vice chairman of his school's DYL branch, he encouraged younger classmates to pursue greater ideological education and organized academic competitions and seminars as well as field trips.

Kim Jong Il graduated from Namsan Higher Middle School in 1960 and enrolled the same year in Kim Il Sung University. He majored in Marxist political economy and minored in philosophy and military science. While at the university, Kim trained as an apprentice in a textile machine factory and took classes in building TV broadcast equipment. During this time, he also accompanied his father on tours of field guidance in several of North Korea's provinces.

Rise to Power

Kim Jong Il joined the Workers' Party, the official ruling party of North Korea, in July 1961. Most political experts believe the party follows the traditions of Stalinist politics even though North Korea began distancing itself from Soviet domination in 1956. The Workers' Party claims to have its own ideology, steeped in the philosophy of Juche. However, in the late 1960s, the party instituted a policy of "burning loyalty" to the "Great Leader" (Kim Il Sung). This practice of personality cult is reminiscent of Stalinist Russia but was taken to new heights with Kim Il Sung and would continue with Kim Jong Il.

Soon after his 1964 graduation from the university, Kim Jong Il began his rise through the ranks of the Korean Workers' Party. The 1960s were a time of high tension between many Communist countries. China and the Soviet Union were clashing over ideological differences that resulted in several border skirmishes, Soviet satellite nations in Eastern Europe were simmering with dissention, and North Korea was pulling away from both Soviet and Chinese influence. Within North Korea, internal forces were attempting to revise the party's revolutionary message. Kim Jong Il was appointed to the Workers' Party Central Committee to lead the offensive against the revisionists and ensure the party did not deviate from the ideological line set by his father. He also led efforts to expose dissidents and deviant policies to ensure strict enforcement of the party's ideological system. In addition, he took on major military reform to strengthen the party's control of the military and expelled disloyal officers.

Kim Jong Il oversaw the Propaganda and Agitation department, the government agency responsible for media control and censorship. Kim gave firm instructions that the party's monolithic ideological message be communicated constantly by writers, artists, and officials in the media. According to official accounts, he revolutionized Korean fine arts by encouraging the production of new works in new media. This included the art of film and cinema. Mixing history, political ideology, and movie-making, Kim encouraged the production of several epic films, which glorified works written by his father. His official biography claims that Kim Jong Il has composed six operas and enjoys staging elaborate musicals. Kim is reported to be an avid film buff who owns more than 20,000 movies, including the entire series of James Bond films, for his personal enjoyment.

Kim Il Sung began preparing his son to lead North Korea in the early 1970s. Between 1971 and 1980, Kim Jong Il was appointed to increasingly important positions in the Korean Workers' Party. During this time, he instituted policies to bring party officials closer to the people by forcing bureaucrats to work among subordinates for one month a year. He launched the Three-Revolution Team Movement, in which teams of political, technical, and scientific technicians traveled around the country to provide training. He was also involved in economic planning to develop certain sectors of the economy.

By the 1980s, preparations were being made for Kim to succeed his father as the leader of North Korea. At this time, the government began building a personality cult around Kim Jong Il patterned after that of his father. Just as Kim Il Sung was known as the "Great Leader," Kim Jong Il was hailed in the North Korean media as the "fearless leader" and "the great successor to the revolutionary cause." His portraits appeared in public buildings along with his father's. He also initiated a series of drop-in inspections of businesses, factories, and government offices. At the Sixth Party Congress in 1980, Kim Jong Il was given senior posts in the Politburo (the policy committee of the Korean Workers' Party), the Military Commission, and the Secretariat (the executive department charged with carrying out policy). Thus, Kim was positioned to control all aspects of the government.

The one area of leadership in which Kim Jong Il might have had a perceived weakness was the military. The army was the foundation of power in North Korea, and Kim had no military service experience. With the assistance of allies in the military, Kim was able to gain acceptance by the army officials as the next leader of North Korea. By 1991, he was designated as the supreme commander of the Korean People's Army, thus giving him the tool he needed to maintain complete control of the government once he took power.

Following the death of Kim Il Sung in July 1994, Kim Jong Il took total control of the country. This transition of power from father to son had never been seen before in a communist regime. In deference to his father, the office of president was abolished, and Kim Jong Il took the titles of general secretary of the Workers' Party and chairman of the National Defense Commission, which was declared the highest office of the state.

Foreign Aid and Nuclear Testing

It is important to understand that much of Kim Jong Il's persona is based on a cult of personality, meaning that legend and official North Korean government accounts describe his life, character, and actions in ways that promote and legitimize his leadership. Examples include his family's nationalist revolutionary roots and claims that his birth was foretold by a swallow, the appearance of a double rainbow over Mount Paekdu, and a new star in the heavens. He is known to personally manage the country's affairs and sets operational guidelines for individual industries. He is said to be arrogant and self-centered in policy decisions, openly rejecting criticism or opinions that differ from his. He is suspicious of nearly all of those who surround him and volatile in his emotions. There are many stories of his eccentricities, his playboy lifestyle, the lifts in his shoes and pompadour hairstyle that make him appear taller, and his fear of flying. Some stories can be verified while others are most likely exaggerated, possibly circulated by foreign operatives from hostile countries.

In the 1990s, North Korea went through a series of devastating and debilitating economic episodes. With the collapse of the Soviet Union in 1991, North Korea lost its main trading partner. Strained relations with China following China's normalization with South Korea in 1992 further limited North Korea's trade options. Record-breaking floods in 1995 and 1996 followed by drought in 1997 crippled North Korea's food production. With only 18 percent of its land suitable for farming in the best of times, North Korea began experiencing a devastating famine. Worried about his position in power, Kim Jong Il instituted the Military First policy, which prioritized national resources to the military. Thus, the military would be pacified and remain in his control. Kim could defend himself from threats domestic and foreign, while economic conditions worsened. The policy did produce some economic growth and along with some socialist-type market practices—characterized as a "flirtation with capitalism"—North Korea has been able to remain operational despite being heavily dependent on foreign aid for food.

In 1994, the Clinton administration and North Korea agreed to a framework designed to freeze and eventually dismantle North Korea's nuclear weapons program. In exchange, the United States would provide assistance in producing two power-generating nuclear reactors and supplying fuel oil and other economic aid. In 2000, the presidents of North Korea and South Korea met for diplomatic talks and agreed to promote reconciliation and economic cooperation between the two countries. The agreement allowed families from both countries to reunite and signaled a move toward increased trade and investment. For a time, it appeared that North Korea was reentering the international community.

Then in 2002, U.S. intelligence agencies suspected North Korea was enriching uranium or building the facilities to do so, presumably for making nuclear weapons. In his 2002 State of the Union address, President George W. Bush identified North Korea as one of the countries in the "axis of evil" (along with Iraq and Iran). The Bush administration soon revoked the 1994 treaty designed to eliminate North Korea's nuclear weapons program. Finally, in 2003, Kim Jong Il's government admitted to having produced nuclear weapons for security purposes, citing tensions with President Bush. Late in 2003, the Central Intelligence Agency issued a report that North Korea possessed one and possibly two nuclear bombs. The Chinese government stepped in to try to mediate a settlement, but President Bush refused to meet with Kim Jong Il one-on-one and instead insisted on multilateral negotiations. China was able to gather Russia, Japan, South Korea, and the United States for negotiations with North Korea. Talks were held in 2003, 2004, and twice in 2005. All through the meetings, the Bush administration demanded North Korea eliminate its nuclear weapons program. It adamantly maintained any normalcy of relations between North Korea and the United States would come about only if North Korea changed its human rights policies, eliminated all chemical and biological weapons programs, and ended missile technology proliferation. North Korea continually rejected the proposal. In 2006, North Korea's Central News Agency announced North Korea had successfully conducted an underground nuclear bomb test.

Failing Health

There have been many reports and claims regarding Kim Jong Il's health and physical condition. In August 2008, a Japanese publication claimed Kim had died in 2003 and had been replaced with a stand-in for public appearances. It was also noted that Kim hadn't made a public appearance for the Olympic torch ceremony in Pyongyang in April 2008. After Kim failed to show up for a military parade celebrating North Korea's 60th anniversary, U.S. intelligence agencies believed Kim to be gravely ill after possibly suffering a stroke. During the fall of 2008, numerous news sources gave conflicting reports on his condition. The North Korean news agency reported Kim participated in national elections in March 2009 and was unanimously elected to a seat in the Supreme People's Assembly, the North Korean parliament. The assembly will vote later to confirm him as chairman of the National Defense Commission. In the report, it was said Kim cast his ballot at the Kim Il Sung University and later toured the facility and talked to a small group of people.

Kim's health was watched closely by other countries because of his volatile nature, the country's possession of nuclear weapons, and its precarious economic condition. Kim also had no apparent successors to his regime, as did his father. His three sons spent most of their lives outside the country and none seemed to be in the favor of the "Dear Leader" to ascend to the top spot. Many international experts believed that when Kim died, there would be mayhem because there seemed to be no apparent method for a transfer of power. But due to the North Korean government's predilection for secrecy, this was too hard to know.

In 2009, however, news reports revealed that Kim planned to name his son, Kim Jong Un as his successor. Very little was known about Kim's heir apparent; until 2010, only one officially confirmed photo of Jong Un existed, and not even his official birthdate had been revealed. The twenty-something was officially confirmed in September 2010.

Kim Jon-Il died December 17, 2011, of a heart attack while traveling on a train. Media reports say the leader was on a work trip for official duties. Upon news of The Dear

Leader's death, North Koreans marched on the capital, weeping and mourning.

Kim is said to be survived by three wives, three sons and three daughters. Other reports claim he has fathered 70 children, most of whom are housed in villas throughout North Korea.

His son, Kim Jong Un, is reported to take up leadership, and the military pledged to support Jong Un's succession.

26 Weird and Bizarre Facts about North Korea that reveal the horrifying truth about life there

Unbelievable Facts.com

North Korea remains among the world's most repressive countries. Under the Kim family's rule, basic freedoms and access to needs have been severely restricted and continue to get frighteningly worse. Akin to Hitler's Germany, North Korea operates secret prison camps where people are violently tortured, abused and forced into hard labour. There is no religious freedom, dissent is silenced through nefarious means and society continues to break down. North Korea shuns the idea of collective co-operation to help itself and others, and may just be a literal hell on earth, isolated as it is from the rest of the world. We bring you 26 weird and bizarre facts about North Korea that will make you thankful that you don't live there.

1.North Korea follows a " three generations of punishment" rule, meaning that if one person violated the law or sent to prison, their children, parents AND grandparents are sent to work with them.

Anyone found guilty of committing a crime (which could be as little as trying to escape North Korea), is sent to the

Kaechon internment camp along with their entire family. The subsequent two generations would be born *in* the camp and must also live their entire lives in servitude and die there.

2. In the 1990's, it was made compulsory for all teachers in North Korea to learn how to play the accordion.

The accordion was often called the 'people's instrument' since it was easy to carry along anywhere. There would be accompanied singing to tunes such as 'We Have Nothing to Envy in the World,' which was a rehash of 'Twinkle, Twinkle Little Star'.

3. A fake propaganda village called Kijong-dong was built in the 1950's after the Korean war to put up the front of a peaceful, prosperous place and to encourage people from the South to defect.

In the last 60 years, over 23,000 North Koreans have defected to South Korea whereas only two South Koreans have gone to the North. According to the North Korean government's official story, Kijong-dong is a collection of multistory buildings that house 200 families who spend their days happily engaging in normal, day-to-day activities. In reality, the buildings' windows have no glasses in them and the electric lights (a luxury that is unheard of to rural North Koreans) are operated on an automatic timer. The only people in sight are maintenance workers who sweep the roads once in a while to give the impression of ongoing activity.

4. Kim Jong-il kidnapped prolific South Korean director Shin Sang-ok and forced him to remake famous Hollywood films in propaganda style.

The kidnap plot was masterminded by Kim Jong-il who was in charge of North Korean film industry before he took up office as the country's leader. He had Shing Sang-ok and the actress Choi Eun-hee kidnapped and the both were kept separate from each other in prison for five years until the former relented. Kim Jong-il's aim was to compel them to create movies that would wow the world. They worked together and produced a series of films, the most notable one being *Pulgasari*, a socialist, propaganda-fueled version of Hollywood's *Godzilla*.

5. North Korea's most popular attraction is visiting Kim Jong-il's preserved body.

The North Korean dictator's embalmed body rests in a state mausoleum and is open for visitation even to foreign tourists. The local guides have a comprehensive knowledge of Kim's life and eagerly point out details about his great achievements and godlike abilities.

6. Elections are held every 5 years in North Korea, but only one name appears on the ballot list. If a voter wishes to choose someone else, they can do so by crossing the name out, but without any anonymity and privacy.

The candidate has a near-100% turnout and the seats are essentially uncompetitive as all of them are chosen and won by the Democratic Front for the Reunification of the Fatherland. Because of this, North Korean elections are termed as "show elections" since they only double as unofficial censuses.

7. Students in North Korea are required to pay for chairs they sit on, the desks they use and the heating fuel during winters.

Shockingly, some students are even made to work producing goods for the government. Parents often bribe the teachers to exempt their kids from this type of hard labour or just don't send them to school, even though it's an act that violates official policy.

8. Human faeces is used instead of fertiliser in North Korea, due to the severe lack of resources. The supply shortage is so extreme that the citizens are FORCED to provide it.

North Korea has zero to none amounts of chemical fertiliser, so the government ordered every person to produce hundreds of kilogrammes of faeces. The faeces is usually mixed with straw and used as a replacement, but the excrement is harder to procure than expected. Cases of theft of squat toilets have been reported, and people have installed locks on their lavatories to prevent this.

9. Kim Jong-un was once caught with a bondage magazine during his school days in Switzerland.

He attended the expensive Liebefeld School near Berne and according to his classmates, was much more interested in football and computer games than his lessons. Also a big fan of Michael Jordan, Kim Jong-un was a good basketball player and was once caught with a bondage magazine in his school bag.

10. It is the year 105 in North Korea, not 2016 because the country marks years from the birth of Kim Il-sung, not Jesus.

North Korea uses the *Juche* calendar, which was introduced in 1997 and is based on Kim Il-sung's date of birth: 15 April 1912. The year 1912 is used as *Juche 1* and there is no *Juche 0*. However, the calendar does maintain the Gregorian calendar's traditional months and the number of days in a month.

11. Distribution, possession and consumption of cannabis is legal in North Korea, and in fact, is recommended as a healthier alternative to tobacco.

According to Sokeel Park, the director of research and strategy at Liberty In North Korea, cannabis grows wildly in North Korea is even sold abroad by government agencies to earn foreign currency. Marijuana is also as good as legal since there is no stigma attached to it and neither is it fetishized as much as it is in the west.

12. In North Korea, the Internet is limited to a very small circle of the elite (only 1,579 IP addresses exist for a population of 25 million). They also have their own operating system called Red Star and the content is pre-filtered by the state.

Red Star is based on Linux and runs a state-approved search engine. Chats, emails, and forum boards are regularly monitored and Internet access in general is only permitted with special authorization and primarily used for government purposes or by foreigners.

13. North Korea enlists around 2000 attractive women as part of a ' Pleasure Squad' who provide entertainment and sexual services for top officials.

The existence of Kim Jong-il's harems has been known to the South Korean intelligence community. According to the account of a Pleasure Squad defector Mi Hyang, groups of young, attractive women were enlisted regularly to provide entertainment and sexual services to top-level government officials.

14. Border relations between North and South Korea are so tense that when soldiers from the South open the door to the North in the Demilitarized Zone, they hold hands to avoid being physically pulled into the other side.

If that doesn't sound crazy enough, here's something. In 2014, South Korean Christians put up a Christmas tree visible from the North Korean Border. North Korea responded by calling it a "tool for psychological warfare" and threatened to bomb it. Bizarrely, North Korea also uses a fax machine to send threats to South Korea.

15. The North Korean regime has long enforced strict rules on styling one's hair; most of the barber shops in Pyongyang advertise photos of government-sanctioned haircuts.

Since Kim Jong-un took power in 2011, the rules have been relaxed a little. It is still preferred that men and women stick to conservative haircuts. Older women can only wear their hair short, whereas the young ones are allowed to sport loose locks, albeit in a neat and cropped fashion. Long hairstyles are generally frowned upon, especially for men.

16. There are an estimated 34,000 statues of Kim Il Sung in North Korea – one for every 3.5 km, or one for every 750 people. All North Koreans are also required to wear a badge featuring his face as a mark of their loyalty to the founder of the nation.

Wearing the badge on their lapels is a daily ritual for everyone and in a city where people rarely carry expensive or valuable items and credit cards, they are highly prized by pickpockets and thieves. So much so, that each badge can be exchanged on the black market for several hundred NKW.

17. Public transportation connecting the main towns is nearly non-existent as citizens need permits to go from one place to another even within the country. Because of this, the streets in North Korea are so empty that children use them as playgrounds and soldiers can be seen hitchhiking on the highways.

In addition to the massive public transport problem, freedom of movement in North Korea is also extremely limited and citizens are rarely allowed to move around freely inside their own country. Cars are strange, foreign things to children and old people that move around on the deserted streets, and often put their lives in danger while crossing the road without looking for oncoming vehicles.

18. A night image of the Korean Peninsula taken by NASA illustrates the sheer isolation and underlying electricity problems in North Korea. Compared to its neighbours South Korea and China, it is completely dark.

Since the defunct Soviet Union stopped supplying power to North Korea in the early 1990's, the country has become entirely energy-bankrupt. Compared to South Korea, where each person consumes 10,162-kilowatt

hours of power, the average North Korean uses just 739. Recently released photos from the International Space Station show how North Korea completely blends into the surrounding blackness, other than a couple of small spots of light.

19. According to data that the government of North Korea provided to the UNESCO, the country's literacy rate is 100% and it boasts that it is on par with the U.S.

With the supposed 100% literacy rate, North Korea ranks equally with the U.S., U.K., and champions hundreds of other countries on that front. According to Asian scholars like Andrei Lankov, this is accomplished by teaching school children how to write the names of "President for Eternity" Kim, Il-sung and "Dear Leader" Kim, Jong-il before they can write their own name and that of their parents'. Once this is done, the North Korean Government declares the student literate in writing. The authenticity of this information still remains to be proved, however.

20. Kim Jong-il was apparently born under a double rainbow and his birth caused a new star to appear in the sky; he learned to walk and talk before 6 months and has the ability to control the weather by his moods, according to the official government-released biography of his life.

An extreme personality cult around the *Kims* exists in North Korea, which even surpasses that of Stalin or Mao Zedong. As part of its propaganda and brain-washing methods, the government elevates its leaders to a godlike status in the minds of the average citizen. One defector, Kang Chol-hwan writes of his childhood in North Korea:

21. Wearing jeans is banned in North Korea as it is seen as a sign of American imperialism.

In a whole slew of restrictions, Kim Jong-un recently issued a ban on jeans and piercings. Pyongyang, the country's elite-infested capital fears that its citizens are being exposed to western clothing, however, the ban will focus primarily on the North Hamgyong province and Yanggang.

22. North Korea is the world's only necrocracy: a government that still operates under the rules of a former, dead leader.

The incumbent president of North Korea is Kim Il-Sung, even though he's been dead for 18 years. He assumed the office of the Eternal Presidency on July 8, 1994, and continues to hold onto power.

23. In 1974, Kim Il-sung took 1,000 Volvo sedans worth € 300M from Sweden to North Korea and never paid for them. They were never returned and are currently still being used.

Tor Rauden Källstigen, a Swedish photographer and entrepreneur who traveled to North Korea in 2008 says,

"Many of the Volvos were put to serve in the small but very present taxi fleet in Pyongyang.I think I've never been inside such an old car even back home in Sweden. This taxi was very well maintained too, close to mint condition it seemed."

The fact remains that despite the semi-annual reminders of payment by the Swedish risk advisory, North Korea refuses to pay for stealing (rather, scamming) Sweden out of the 1,000 volvos. North Korea now considers Sweden a US pawn that is manipulated by the imperialists.

24. In North Korea, possessing Bibles, watching South Korean movies and distributing pornography may be punishable by death.

In November of 2013, the government executed 80 people in public for watching South Korean movies and owning Bibles. According to one source, women and children were brought into a sports stadium and forced to watch people being shot dead by machine-gun fire. Despite it being illegal, it is estimated that there are 100,000 Christians living in North Korea.

25. North Koreans don' t celebrate birthdays on July 8 and December 17, since those are the dates that Kim Il-sung and Kim Jong-il died.

Approximately 100,000 North Koreans celebrate displaced birthdays on July 9 or December 18 due to this reason. There is a provision for people born on these dates before 1994, where they can change their birthday with official recognition.

26. The national animal of North Korea is the Chollima; a mythical winged horse that supposedly symbolizes heroism and the country' s indomitable spirit.

The word Chollima is derived from the Chinese word Qianlima which means talent and ability. This mythical winged horse actually originates from Chinese classics. The national capital Pyongyang hosts a number of Chollima statues, and strangely enough, the North Korean football team is also named the same.

Chapter One

Honolulu, Hawaii

The early morning breeze pushed the lingering fog from the night before through the jogging path. Jamie kept her stride, so Ziggy could keep up. She stopped, "Ziggy, come on boy." She tried to coach him, but he had been intrigued by something. He sniffed until he found a trail through a bush. He came out when he heard his name, looked at her with great concern.

"Boy, if you don't bring your rump here." She wiped her sweat, fanned her face, and went to pick him up, but he ran into the bushes. "Oh my God, are you serious." Frustrated, she went after him, almost having his tail, "When I get my hands on you." She was dirty from the fall to her knees, scratches from the thorny bushes.

He barked, just out of reach of her fingers; it was almost like he was pulling her closer to where he had been. Just on the other side of this huge leaf, she reached in as hard as she could, grabbed him by the tail. "What the hell are you…" she looked up, not far from where she stood, not believing what she was watching. She covered her mouth to prevent her scream from being heard. "No!" she held Ziggy tight, "Please stop!" She wanted to run, but her feet inched closer, her eyes pooled with fear, "Stop! Please don't hurt him."

Before she knew it, she was closer to the men that were beating a man with objects as he hung from a tree, the screams for help quickly went silent when his mouth was stuffed with a white towel. She could not understand how they ignored her plea. From the corner of his eye, he tried to tell her to run. The blood and wounds that puffed his face was unbearable.

She woke up from this reoccurring dream, breathing hard, chest pounded like she had been running. She reached over and slammed her palm on the alarm clock that woke her up. She wanted to know why her dreams were so vivid; it was as if she was really there. She sighed, grabbed her cell and noticed three missed calls from her boyfriend, "Damn, I got to get going." She jumped up, tossed her panties and bra on as she made her way to the rest room. Her cell rang, with her toothbrush in her mouth, "Hello."

"Hey gorgeous, were you sleeping?" he waited in line to pass through customs.

"Matter of fact I was, but I'll meet you at your house" They both ended the call.

"Excuse me sir, can you please accompany me to my office?" A soft voice came from behind. His nerves started to bother him. But it wasn't unusual under these circumstances.

"Well..." He stuttered. "Sure, why not." He spoke with a smile, and wiped the perspiration from his forehead and wondered if they would notice his hands. She looked at his airline ticket.

"Mr. Kalargo Choi, do you have your passport?" The customs agent asked. He held all his emotions under control, just like he had practiced.

"Well certainly. It should be in my carry-on bag, the side
pocket."

He thought to himself and wondered about the consequences. He looked around and saw himself in the reflection. He sighed. "What did I get myself into?"

He saw a small particle on his shoulder, and immediately removed it with his left hand as if it was illegal. He wore Levi's jeans neatly ironed with a blue polo pull over, and a pair of black ostrich ankle high boots. Mr. Choi stood no more than 5'10, two hundred fifteen pounds. He was a handsome Gambian who is as ebony as jet ink. He was well built physically and mentally due to years of jiujutsu martial arts, that was accompanied with a third degree black belt. At this moment, customs are the only people he feared.

"Mr. Choi, where are you arriving from?"The customs officer asked him.

He responded quickly. "I'm arriving from South Africa." He remembered to not add anything to the conversation between the two.

"Are you a citizen of the United States of America?"

"Yes I am." He breathed lightly to ease his nerves.

"How long have you been in South Africa?"

He looked mystified for a split second. "No more than a month." He plunged his pinky finger in his left ear.

"Are you transporting any illegal drugs, weapons, or any items that would be contraband?" the customs agent placed his hands on top of his bags.

"No I'm not." He spoke with confidence.

"Are you carrying a large amount of cash that you have

not declared on your customs sheet?" He looked at the ceiling and quickly returned eye contact.

"No sir."
"Are you bringing back any gifts?"

He shook his head. "No sir." He removed a tear of sweat with his right pinky finger. At the same time the customs officer went through his luggage, and took out the obvious. They searched carefully, one item at a time.

"What is this?" He asked.

"I'm sorry. I made that myself upon arriving in South Africa. Is that considered a gift?" He frowned.

The officer gave him an innocent pout. He looked at him, "Not really, I guess not. It's mighty small."

"Where do you reside in the U.S.?"

He was day dreaming and did not hear him.

"Excuse me sir, I asked you a question. Where do you live in the U.S.?"

He responded, "Honolulu."

"What's your occupation?"

He smiled, "I'm a martial arts instructor, a personal trainer and I own import/export business."

The officer looked him in the eyes with his passport in his hand, "Welcome back to the U.S, be careful of the heavy snow in the mountains at this time of the year. You may proceed. Pack your clothes." He said with a steady stare.

Kalargo returned the stare and finally relaxed to a mood of safety and comfort. He sighed with a password. "Tell the people who are visiting Hawaii about the snow." He packed his bags.

"Why this can't be any easier?" He was still nervous as hell.

He stood in front of a mirror in the airport bathroom and removed all signs of perspiration and guilt. He perfected his gig line up with his belt. Finally he combed his hair with an Afro pick.

He walked toward the exit with his luggage in tow, pulled out his cell phone, from memory he dialed Na Min's number and waited.

"Yes hello." A female voice responded in fluent Korean.

"Yes, Na Min." The phone went silent for a moment.

"Yes, He'll be right with you."

He walked toward the limo stand. The Hawaiian heat embraced his face like an old friend who had not seen him in years. He could see the afternoon sun hovering over the horizon. He smiled. "Damn, I'm glad to be back."

A voice interrupted him. "Kalargo, how was your trip?"

He laughed with a joyful voice. "Just great, could not be better.

Na Min had a Korean accent when he spoke English. "Where are you now?"

"Waiting for my driver, I should be home in about forty five minutes."

"Well I'm glad to know you are back and safe, call me later." after a couple more words, they both terminated the line and he placed the phone in his top left pocket.

The driver pulled up alongside him, he tossed his bags in the car, and departed Honolulu International airport to get on the Queen Liliuokalani freeway, he pondered his first day he came to Hawaii and most of all, and how he got to South Korea.

At the age of nine, he lived in The Gambia. Unknown to his knowledge, he was in hiding. He and his uncle lived in a shack under a tin roof. They barely ate four complete meals a week. Mugumbi, his uncle has been taking care of him for the past five years. After he was laid off from the diamond mine, they struggled for weeks until he found work at the docks. He loved ships and saw them as the beast of the sea. Later he found a way out of Africa, a way to riches. As usual Kalargo was in the streets while his uncle continued to work hard and planed their great escape.

After three years, his plan came to him in the middle of the night. The next morning he woke up with a smile.

"Good morning little one, it's time to open your eyes and smell the sunshine." He literally meant the humidity including the outstanding stench that floated among them like a friend, a dirty friend or worst a flatulent ghost with murderous intentions. They lived in a small-cemented center block efficiency, half kitchen with an outside bathroom. There was one thing that they had in common and it only occurred in the middle of the night, their dreams, and they ended when their eyelids opened and allowed reality to piss in their face.

"Tipi, it's time to eat, so go ahead and wash your face, he would've added brushing his teeth to the list of things to do but neither owned one." This time he spoke with a little more authority in his voice. The nickname Tipi stuck to Kalargo every since he was younger. Most of his family had been killed and leaving to get away from the genocide was the last option. But somehow and a mysterious reason, it was like they followed them. The house bombing nearly killed him. A huge gash on the side of his neck was a reminder.

He lay on the floor between a dirty sheet and blanket. Surprisingly, his eyes flickered to keep out the early morning sunlight. He yawned to get himself started.

"It's early." Neither of them spoke English nor read or write their own language.

"This week…" He said with a smile. "I have big plans for the both of us. But you have to promise me…" He bent down beside him on the floor. He lifted his chin to look him directly in his eyes. He licked his thumb to wet it real good, wiped the dried saliva and eye snot from the corners of his face. Hardly awake he sat up right and looked into his uncle's eyes.

"What's the happiness for?" Before he could finish, his uncle spoke.

"Promise me you'll never say a word! One day you and I will be out of here, just wait you'll see."

Kalargo couldn't believe the words that suddenly became melodic.

"Do you promise not to say a word to no one?"

He was so hungry, he would promise anything at this moment, "I promise, but what are you talking about?" He looked like he was begging for food and lost.

"When the time come, I'll let you know. From this day on, just be happy and don't ask or mention this conversation again." He knew it would be hard to be happy under these conditions, if he had a plan, it must be a good one.

After six months of waiting, He started to wonder. "Uncle..." He began to say with an inquisitive voice. He stood between the door way of their shack. He leaned with his left hand on his hip. The humidity made him melt like ice cream and his upper lip tasted salty, sticky sweat that wet his shirt. His uncle stared out and down the street admiring what he hoped to never see again.

The next-door neighbor exited her house. "Hello, how is it going?"

"Fabulous, just like a garden of roses." he said as she walked across the street carrying a pot on top of her head filled with clothes. She mumbled under her breath.

"Yep, He's getting crazier and crazier. Just look at him." She smiled at him. They used to date. But everything had changed. He hadn't been with a woman in six months. But no one could tell from his gestures.

Tipi approached him with a sad pout. He took up the space between the door and his uncle. Nothing had changed, not even the scuba tight pants. It drove him insane. People in the neighborhood began to call his uncle crazy behind his back.

"Tipi..." He paused for a second that felt like a lifetime. He held his face in his palms to hide his pain.

"Tipi…" He put his hands on his right shoulder. "…how would you like to come with me to work tonight? At least you won't be bored." He sighed, "You know Tipi, tonight is that night." He whispered.

Kalargo's head lifted slowly. These were the best words he had ever heard. Before he replied, his uncle interrupted him.

"We are leaving tonight. I've been waiting six months, six damn months!" A tear fell out of joy.

"Tipi, say good bye to Africa. You may never return."

His heartbeat began to race. He wanted to dream, scream and celebrate at the same time. He also remembered to keep calm.

Mugumbi's plan was to travel to the United States by ship as a stowaway. Only if the ship they had boarded was going to America. Due to his inability to read, they boarded a ship with an American flag that ended up in South Korea. After months of working under the table for slave wages, Mugumbi finally got a break. He met his future Korean American wife that introduced him to a prestigious individual, her stepfather, double agent Na Min Choi.

Kalargo's driver was steady talking, not realizing that his mind was far away until they pulled up to the gate of his house.

He retrieved his PDA cell phone and used it to open the remote controlled gate. She drove up the driveway in the Hawaiikai section of Honolulu.

"Home sweet home…" He dialed Na Min's number.

He walked in to his home with the cell phone to his ear. "Good after noon. Mr. Choi, please."

He tossed his bags on the bed and pulled off his shirt and threw it in the basket of dirty clothes.

"Kalargo, are you feeling pretty good?"

He lay on the bed, tired. "I was wondering if we could meet later tonight and…"

Kalargo interrupted him "Well, hold on for a moment. I have to check my schedule", he came back. "Of course I have time."

He stood up, unclothed himself and prepared his bath water.

"I say after ten pm." The sound of bath water can be heard in the back ground.

"You want to meet at Nicolis Nicolis?"

"Sure, why not. So ten it is." They ended the conversation.

The huge bathroom covered with ivory pearl tile displayed a checkerboard design, ivory white sink and brass facets handles. The lit watermelon candles and bubble bath was exactly what he needed, relaxation. The Jacuzzi's pumps massaged his back while he closed his eyes under dim lights. He thought of how successful he wanted to be. He already owned one of the most popular martial arts and fitness spas on the island. But the bulk of his money came from international arms trade and distribution, sound fancy. In reality, he supplied war torn countries weapons to fight. On his list was his native country The Gambia that was in need of his service.

The phone rang several times. "Who is bothering me now?" He opened his eyes and reached for the phone. "Yes who's calling?"

His thick African accent could not be mistaken for anything other than a Gambian. He splashed water that can be heard in the background. He paused for a second or two.

"Hello." He said just before he pushed the button to end the call. He heard a female voice. It sounded like Jamie.

"I heard you playing with your rubber ducky." She said in a seductive voice that purred in his ear. He laughed and blew off her comment, in one ear and out the other.

"I thought you were my rubber ducky? Having fun?" With her lips she made this sound that always excited him. He raised himself forward to pull the plug to the drain.

"Jamie, Could you call me back or I'll call you." He asked her. He hopped out of the deep Jacuzzi to dry off. She hesitated before she responded.

"You promise?"

"Well I tell you what; you call me in fifteen minutes. I should be dry by then." She agreed and they terminated the line.

The Hawaiian nights are what people enjoy, but the sun and beaches are what they come for. The weather attracted tourist from all parts of the globe. He rarely left the island. He was glad to be home. He lounged in his four-bedroom house surrounded by a seven-foot wall in one of the exclusive neighborhoods in Hawaii.

He entered the kitchen to prepare a snack. He wore his favorite white cotton robe, blue pajamas and slippers that matched. His house was built to look and have an Oriental appeal. His admiration for the Korean was evident. He ate with chopsticks like they were born in his hand.

There was nothing he did not know. He cooked their food more and better than Gambian. But he had a slightly different taste bud when it came to women. He had grown to be this debonair that he had dreamed of. He lived in Hawaii for ten years. He was lonely and missed his only family, Mugumbi.

He opened the fridge. "Well now…" He looked at baked chicken, noodles and a plate jeon. He grabbed a little of everything just to satisfy all his taste buds. He spoke out loud. "I guess a little red wine…" He tuned out loud. "…should not hurt the mind, at least not this time."

He grabbed a flute shaped glass walked into the living room under dim lights. He picked up the remote control.

"Hmm…" With one touch, the wall unit rose from the floor and the entertainment center appeared.

"Do I want to watch T.V., listen to jazz?" He hit the music button, "may be some Jazz." He flopped in to the colossal circular black sofa.

"Spanish Jazz, I 'm in the mood for." He looked at his watch and noticed it was nearly eight thirty. He picked up the phone to call Jamie. The ring tone buzzed his ear and his eyes watched the EQ on the stereo, jazz filtered the entire house.

"Hello this is Jamie…" Kalargo sighed. "Hey what's

up? You are kind of late calling." He was interrupted with a rueful voice.

"Can you hold?" It caught him off guard and he had to wait a moment. She finally came back with this cheerful voice.

"I am so sorry, who is this?" Like a dummy he spoke in to the machine.

"This is Kalargo."

"I am not in at the moment. Please leave a short to the point message. I'll get a hold of you verbally, mentally, physically, or joyfully. Thank you." He grinned.

"She gets me every time. Yeah Jamie, I call to say hello and to return your call..." A buzzer interrupted him. He stood up to check his monitor.

"Anyway just call me" He slid the phone in his robe pocket.

"Are you going to let me in?" Jamie stood at the gate camera. She hopped in to her car.

"Of course, park your car next to the Lexus. Make sure to be careful, I just had the roses planted."

Jamie stood 5'7, long curly blonde hair with a pecan like tan with crystal sky blue eyes. Jamie was born in San Diego and lived on the island ever since her parents separated. Upon meeting him, she worked at a fruit market for three years on the side of the road in an unpopulated section of the island.

After she parked her car, she double-checked to make certain there was space between the Lexus.

"How's it?" She said and embraced him and pushed her tongue down his throat.

"Well, you know as usual."

"Come on in, I'm having a glass of wine. She made herself comfortable. She sat her black purse on the sofa and sighed like she had never been there before.

"So how was your flight?" She chose a champagne glass.

"You want champagne or wine?" He held a bottle of each in both hands.

"I'll have whatever you are having." She held her glass up and watched the wine pour. She looked at him with cunning gesture and sipped a little before she took her glass to the sofa and sat down like a lady.

"My day was boring. I arrived on the afternoon flight; actually it was delayed due to a layover in the Philippines. Other than that I was listening to some Jazz."

"So how is your dad?" She crossed her legs.

"Actually He's doing fine. I am meeting him tonight. What are you doing later? He would love to see you." He sat next to her. She watched T.V. with her glass touching her lips. "Nothing really, I wanted to spend some time with you."

He stood up and looked at his watch. "I guess you wouldn't mind coming with me to meet him?" He headed toward the master suite but can be heard. "Then we can go to the beach afterwards."

"Should I change my clothes?" She sat the glass on the table, stood from the sofa and entered the kitchen.

"You know I like to go to the beach, especially at night." He came from the master suite "Yati yati yati, we both know why you like the beach."

She was in front of the open fridge picking grapes from the bag. She tossed a couple of them in her mouth. Suddenly he came from behind with a loving embrace. He put his lips on the back of her neck. His body pressed against hers.
She wore a pair of skintight jeans that made her look luscious. She grinds her buttocks into his mid section.

"Now you know you like to tease and keep me hungry for you." She looked over her shoulder.

"Why would I…" The ringing of his cellular phone interrupted her.

"What time is it?" He asked looking down at his watch.

"Nine fifteen." He sighed.

"Yes hello." He walked away from Jamie. The voice on the phone quickly put a smile on his voluptuous lips. He moved far enough to talk in private.

"So how is it going on your end?" The voice asked him.

"Very well, I sent the package. It should arrive in less than four hours. The commander is part of the flight crew. He should be contacting you one hour after they land to inform you where to meet him." he walked into an unoccupied part of the house and then entered his office.

"Everything is cool but what about the other crew

members?"

"Like I said, everything is under control. Nobody else knows a thing. It's what they call TOP SERCET. We are taking this seriously."

"Well, until then I'll wait on the call and I'll be near the base in a couple of hours. I'll talk to you later, out." They both ended the phone call.

Chapter 2

The blazing sun glared on the ocean that made a mirror reflection. It was amazing how beautiful and calm a huge body of water could be. The Indian Ocean can be lonely at times but once in a while the calm and peaceful waters are disturbed by an U.S.S. aircraft carrier.

The U.S.S. Carl Vinson operated a hundred miles off the island of Diego Garcia, population six hundred; the island was three miles wide and twenty-eight miles long. One of the beautiful islands that Great Britain owned and not known to many. It was used as a military installation.

The battle group cruised towards the North Arabian Sea. It carried a crew of five thousand and over fifty aircraft of various squadrons. Squadron VRC-50 was the most love and expected aircraft to land. The twin turbo prop C-2 better known as the GREYHOUND delivered passengers, parts, and most important, mail. Its day or night, long range capabilities and any weather were perfect for Naval Logistics. The squadron was stationed out of Cubi Point Naval Air station, Philippines. The squadron detached personnel aboard the carrier to assist in logistics. The sound of a C-2 was like x-mas every time.

"Good morning, how does the flight deck look?" The leading Petty Officer entered the small cramped workspace crowded with toolboxes and six sailors waiting to recover an aircraft.

"Well, the ETA says fourteen hundred hours but we got to have it ready for the next flight cycle.

A voice mumbled out. "Ok it's thirteen thirty now. In about ten minutes. I want to be up on the flight deck and ready. I don't want the air boss breathing down my neck and chewing my ass out for not recovering are own bird. He took a seat on the edge of the desk.

"Airman Crockett, do a quick turnaround. It doesn't have to be too thorough, just look for the obvious and write it down. I know it's your first time out at sea. And you are the plane captain but out here we are one team, one family. We pitch in. Basically, we don't do major maintenance out here unless we absolutely have to. If you find something, let me know, write it down. We'll let the crew back on land handle it. Oh by the way, make sure you put your order in for whatever you need from base." He sat there like a big shot with goggles on the top of his cranial like a tank commander.

"The other squadrons don't mind helping us out with supplies only because we do them favors. So stock supplies for the minor problems."

His dingy olive green fatigues were tucked in his unpolished boots. A crew of six included an aviation mechanic, structural/hydraulic, electrician, avionics, plane captain, and a Q/A quality and assurance, just enough to get the job done.

"Did they say what they were carrying?" Airman Crockett asked while sitting on top of a toolbox holding a pair of gloves in his hand. He looked like he was expecting his Japanese girlfriend to jump out of a birthday cake.

"Well I'm not sure but I do know they have about ten passengers and two weeks of backed up mail." The leading Petty Officer said.

Airman Crockett stood 5'9, twenty years old with a military haircut, a hundred seventy pounds, an African American from Miami Florida. He just arrived to the squadron eight months ago.

"Well it's about that time." The leading Petty Officer headed out the iron integrity door of the ship. The workspace was located just below the flight deck, starboard aft section. There is a sixty-foot drop into the ocean if anyone wanted to free dive. Not like it has not been done before by lonely sailors who are in desperate need to go home. The catwalk was made of iron and it lead to the flight deck. You could hear and see the waves that splashed against the side of the ship through the iron that was beneath your feet.

The catapult can be felt as it launches the fighter jets and bombers. Even with ear protection you can barely hear the person next to you screaming in your ear. The use of hand signals told everyone when, what, and where to go on the flight deck. The fumes that hovered the mini airport from more than fifteen planes at any given time are just as dangerous. The exhaust from any one of them could blow you off the flight deck into the ocean, worst-case scenario, to be blown into the engine of another plane.

Petty Officer, E-7, the quality assurance officer and leader of the detachment, the career type was born in Paris, Texas, a country fellow that spoke with a deep drawl. His is a dishwater blonde red head that stood 5'11, two hundred thirty pounds. The Petty Officer walked over to Airman Crockett.

"Now look, the air boss want the C-2 parked next to the island of the aircraft carrier, just below the flight control center. You won't be shutting the engines down. They will unload and take off. Ok?" He screamed in his direction of his earmuff. He spoke over the loud engines that were at high power six feet away.

"There she is." The C-2 was pointed out circling the ship in between the high clouds; it looked like a flying dot. It did donuts around the carrier waiting for its chance to land. There is no other aircraft that looked as dangerous as the wide fat big nose short C-2 landing on the flight deck. You have to imagine the ship shifting left to right and up and down according to motion of the ocean. Then the C-2 Greyhound trying to land, believe me, it is a sight to see. And do not forget about the wind that drifts the plane as it tries to land.

As the plane approached for landing, the flight deck firemen and other crew members were on standby. Not more than one mile out, it took the last fly by before it descended. The C-2 lined up with lighting that guided the plane in. A long trail of exhaust smoke lingered behind the turbo prop as it struggled to line itself for landing. It looked like it would crash into the ocean or the ship.

"On deck! On deck!" The flight deck loud speaker said. The plane quickly full throttled in case they missed four of the landing cables they have in place to catch them. The tail hook lifted, and they taxied to the island. Not more than two minutes later an F-14 landed and the process continued.

After unloading passengers and mail the leading Petty Officer sent a crew member to the workspace with two unbelievable flat boxes two and a half by fifteen inches.

"What! Pizza Hut! Hot damn, Pizza Hut in the middle of the ocean! Where did that come from?" Airman Crockett yelled.

"It came from where we are going next..." Petty Officer Ramsey yelled back, "...North Arabian Sea?" The guy smiled and walked off, "War baby."

The C-2 was directed to the catapult and ready for takeoff. Like a slingshot it was thrown off the front of the ship at a minimum of one hundred fifty miles per hour.

Moments later, the phone rang in the VRC-50 workspace. They had slices of pizza in their mouths and gobbling like wild turkeys.

"VRC-50 this is a non secure line how can I help you sir or maim?" P.O. Ramsey had licked his lips and fingers while holding the phone with shoulder.

"This is the air boss, did they deliver the pizza?"

"Yes sir, it should be there. It's already in route."

"Tell your crew, job well done..." he added a couple of more words and ended the call.

Several hours had passed and the sun was swallowed by the horizon that made a cloudless night filled with stars. At any given time you could make a wish to a fallen star. Airman Crockett looked out into the pitch darkness knowing that only the battle group was near. Flight operations went on until 2200 hours.

"Well, it's about that time to hit the rack." He looked at his watch and sighed. "We don't have to be up until what, 1330 hours?" He looked at the POD the plan of the day to verify when the next C-2 will arrive.

The voice of the Captain of the ship bellowed the speaker of the 1-M-C that the entire ship can hear. "This is the Captain, I would like to have everyone's attention for a moment. Today was a fine working day. Currently I would like to give an AT a Boy to squadron VF-120 and VA-140 for doing an excellent job on their bomb runs. It carried out expeditiously without injuries. However we all know that we all work as a team, a ship is nothing without its crew. I also know that it is a little hard on some of us being away from family and love ones for such a long period of time. In three days it'll be Christmas and…" The captain paused. "Yes it's a difficult time. But we are out here making sure the international sea lanes are open and not controlled by countries whom wish to do harm or take over countries that can't take up for themselves. So yes, as the most powerful country in the world, we have a job to do, an obligation to protect international waters." He cleared his throat and continued.

"I just got word today that our mission has changed. The chief of Naval Operations has given us the orders to be on standby due to Saddam Hussein's Army attacking Kuwait. At this very moment we are full speed ahead to the Persian Gulf in which is now called the Arabian Sea."As the Captain spoke Airman Crockett could feel mood change among his crew. It humbles some; it got serious all of a sudden. He wondered, will this be war? He had noticed weeks earlier that they had replenished the carrier with bombs and the practice flights had increased dramatically. He also remembered that another group of his squadron was detached to Manama, Bahrain, fifty miles from Saudi Arabia and three hundred miles from Kuwait. He knew that was within scud missile range. He thought about the threat of gas attacks and chemical suits. He shook his head and sighed. The buildup of more battle groups were being positioned and there were two battle groups already there, U.S.S. Midway, U.S.S. Enterprise. He thought about what the President of the United States said, "War is eminent."

*   *   *

Two weeks later, under an unforgiving blistering sun that made sweat feel like boiling water on the flight deck with high powered exhaust hot enough to melt your skin beneath a brown turtle neck sweater. Airman Crockett carried a set of three chains to secure the C-2 to the flight deck to prevent the plane from shifting when the ship rocks and roll. The leading Petty Officer walked over to him.

"Hey after you secure the C-2 we have a meeting, so don't disappear.

"What's the meeting about?"

"We have to go over our tools and get ready to take off. We are flying to Bahrain first thing in the morning. The bird is spending the night. So after we go over some details as a group, be ready for a catapult take off."

"Damn flying off the ship." he sighed.

Later that night he barely slept because he could not stop thinking about this catapult take off. He had seen it many times and now, he has to experience it. He felt like the C-2 Greyhound now looked like a flying coffin instead of looking like a friendly snoopy. He slept in a coffin rack that was the size of a real coffin, may be seven feet long by three feet wide. The berthing quarters stacked the coffin like beds three up and three in front of him, very small space where he have to lift his bed to put all of his belongings. If it doesn't fit, you don't need it.

The 0430 wakeup call was a tapping noise on the edge of the rack. "It is that time." A fellow crew member gave him a wakeup call.

"Do I have time to eat?" He asked with a war ending breath that he covered with the sheet.

"We have box lunches ready for us on the plane. The in flight plane captain has already pick those up, by the way have you ever taken off from an aircraft carrier?"

"No." He peeked through the sheets that had covered his head.

"Well there is a first time for everything." He walked away with a grin.

The C-2 had to be the slowest aircraft the Navy has. The flight was like riding a snail with wings. It would take a fighter thirty minutes to fly from where the ship was located. The C-2 took two hours and thirty minutes to arrive in Bahrain. Airman Crockett closed his eyes and thought about the very first time he landed in a foreign country.

Eight months ago

The night was hot, humid, and beautiful at the same time. He knew he was in a whole new world. The people were different by culture, language, habit, and much more. The Philippine women, you could not ask for any more exotic. The short, dark skin almond eyes with jet-black hair and their accent, was mind blowing. He was dropped into heaven without a white flag.

"Have you heard about the game called QUARTERS?" A passenger asked him.

"This guy knows where all the good spots to go to, you coming?"

He frowned, "Naa, You guys go without me. I already know about QUARTERS."

His dream was interrupted when the in flight plane captain shook his shoulder.

"We are landing in five minutes." He went around waking up everyone who was sleeping.

He sighed and opened his eyes. He looked out the window and
saw dessert for miles. "Wow! Now this is a whole new world."

*   *   *

Honolulu, Hawaii

Jamie slept through the night having the same horrific dream. She mumbled words that Kalargo ignored until she almost gagged. In her dream she was jogging on a trail like she usually does.

"I'm going jogging along the trail. I'll be back within the hour." She spoke into her answering machine. She exited the house wearing her red tights and white t-shirt with a pouch around her waist. She went back in to the house to change her batteries for her walk man head set. She also grabbed her best cassette tape, Phil Collins.

"Where are you?" she called and whistled for her cute annoying black chiwawa with a little bit of brown on its belly. Ziggy ran from the pet entrance of the door that swung both directions.

"Come on Ziggy. It's time for our morning run. He wagged his tail and moved around like he had been waiting on her the whole time. He jumped in to the grass from the porch and took his ritual pump and morning dump. After he finished he turn around to smell it, licked it, and backed away from it.

It was a perfect morning to jog under a cloudless sky with pockets of fog that looked like they floated just above the ground along the green grassy trail. Some people referred to Jamie as a health addict and others just labeled her as drop dead gorgeous.

After a mile and a half her heartbeat was at a normal joggers beat on a trail that she jogged at least three times a week. She arrived at her turn around point and noticed that Ziggy was not behind her. She stopped and removed her headphones. She began to trace backwards.

"Ziggy!" She yelled out his name. She listened. Suddenly Ziggy came from the bushes.

"There you are!" She was relieved. But Ziggy stood there and looked into the bushes. He wagged his tail and barked two times. The closer she got, the further he would go into the bushes. She sighed.

"I don't have time for this. Come on boy." She begged him.

Ziggy peaked out of a small hole between the bushes like he was calling her, as soon as she got closer. He took off behind the bushes again. It was like a game he played.

When she walked through the bushes and pulled huge leaves aside to make her way. She saw a black man hanging upside down from a tree. His blood dripped like a faucet, and his face was swollen like water balloons. She grabbed her chest with her right hand and covered her mouth with her left. It was as if the two guys that beat him mercifully could not see her standing there. The body moved on every strike until they stop beating him. She walked closer with tears in her eyes, "Stop! What are you doing?" She asked them.

They ignored her like she was invisible. The closer she got, the more she realized that she was like a ghost.

She dropped to her knees and pleaded the two soldiers to stop beating him.
"You are going to kill him!" She screamed from the bottom of her lungs and pulling on her shirt like she was going to rip it off.

"What are you doing?!" She reached for his hand.

His eyes opened as blood spilled from his mouth like a gutted pig. She crawled over to him and grabbed his bloody hand that barely touched the dirt that had mixed together. She squeezed his hand tight.

"Wake up Jamie! Hey, you must be having a bad dream." He held her hand.
Her eyes opened wide and she jumped away from him like he was the attacker.

"Are you going to be ok?" He sighed and got her a glass of water.

She looked around with sweat on her forehead. She scratched her chest and rubbed her nose. Her blood shot wet eyes made her realized that she was safe, but her scratches on her chest and the tears from the corner of her eyes said otherwise.

"My God," She swallowed a dry throat of saliva, "was I talking in my sleep?" She asked him.

"What! You were mumbling and moaning something, looked like you were having a…" He was interrupted. "…A nightmare on Elm Street." He laughed and gave her some water.

"What were you dreaming about?"

"I…" She sighed. "I can't remember." She paused and cuddled with him.

"I can't believe I do not know what I was dreaming about. I'm pretty sure it will come to me sooner or later." She lay there with his favorite white robe on with nothing else beneath. Her beautiful lips and facial features gave her a VIP passed to anywhere.

"Hold me." He kissed her on the neck and embraced her.

"Are you hungry? I cooked breakfast while you were sleeping."

She inhaled and smelt fresh eggs and bacon.

"Yes, love to eat" She stood up and tightened the robe around
her. His beeper went off. He looked down and picked up the phone.

"I tell you what…" She walked into the kitchen. "…I'll fix my plate, you answer your beeper." She grabbed two

52

plates for them both.

Chapter 3

"Na Min, what's going on? I am surprise to hear from you this early."

"Good morning to you too, I think we have a problem. The shipment we got several weeks ago."

Kalargo is outside opening his car door. "What about it?"

He heard him sigh, "All of that has to be shipped out. There is another shipment coming in tomorrow. From what I understand, it needs to go ASAP." He became quiet.

He was caught by surprise. He pondered while he sat in his car. "Does it have to be done tonight?" He sounded like a kid on punishment. "My contact is not able to move anything right now. I have no way to get trucks." He rubbed his left pinky finger on his left collarbone below where his scar was.

"The ship will be docked in the harbor. The name is "RUSH" Captain Tomzach will be expecting your arrival three hours prior to their departure. If you have to rent the trucks, do it. We have people counting on this."

Kalargo spoke and thought at the same time, "Tell them handyman is on the move." They ended the call.

He looked in the rear view mirror to pick a fight with a painful nose hair. Then he quickly dialed a number from memory.

"Bennett, yeah good morning, wake up. Hey I know you can hear me."

A voice responded. "What are you doing calling me so early?" He coughed and spat in to the trash.

"We got work to do tonight." He explained.

"What time is it?" He laid his head in to the pillow.

"It's Ten am but by ten tonight, we need to have everything loaded on the dock."

Bennett stopped him, "Tonight! I thought…"

"I know what you thought, I said the same thing. Grab ten of your guys, don't worry they will be paid well as usual. Because of the short notice, I will rent the trucks."

He sighed with his head under the pillow with the phone to his mouth. "I guess I could be ready in a couple of hours." He tried to hang up the phone but Kalargo got a couple of last words in.

"I'll call you at six o'clock on the dot. Have them ready." The line went dead.

Jamie tiptoed towards the car like she was modeling on top of hot stones for a pageant with no shoes on.

"Your breakfast is getting cold. Did you want milk or orange juice?" She leaned forward with her hands on her knees still in his robe.

"Orange juice." They both walked hand in hand in to the house.

*   *   *

"Yes I would like to speak to Zang please."

Na Min stood 5'6 with a receding hairline and gray streaks that blended among his straight hair that touched his shoulder. He was an expert in computer programming, and the gathering of Tactical Intelligence. He spoke four languages and held a black belt in martial arts. He trained Kalargo in his younger days. Because he was a Korean American and spoke Korean it gave him an ability to be a good spook until he turned. He was born in Korea raised in Seattle. At the age of thirty he became a leading Agent and a double Agent for the North Koreans. He had moved so far up the ladder. He had frequent meetings with the President of the United States to personally inform him of the North Koreans nuclear technology advancement, troop movement, and activities. But what Agent Na Min did not inform him on was their activities outside the borders of the North Korean peninsula.

"Yes Na Min, How is it going in Hawaii?" Zang spoke in Korean.

"I am calling to inform you that the equipment should be on the move tonight. Now you said the next load should be in tomorrow. But nothing changes, right?" he waited for his response.

"That will be right. I know this is premature; however I

55

am sorry for the short notice. Everything's going well..."
Agent Na Min was interrupted.

"How's the weather?" Zang asked. They both grinned.

*   *   *

Kalargo's house

The whole house smelt like fried eggs, bacon and sausages that floated pass their noses.

"Tell me when too much." She put eggs on the plate until he held his hand up to signal that's enough. He tossed a couple of strips of bacon, and sausages on the plate and parked his rear end on the sofa. They watched T.V. and enjoyed each other's company.

"Is there any more apple juice?" He spoke with a piece of bacon between his teeth and talking at the same time.

"Actually I had the last glass of apple juice last night. Only thing left is orange juice, grapefruit, and milk." She looked in the fridge with a half of sausage in her right hand and the other half in her mouth.

"Mix orange juice and fruit punch." he requested. She frowned like that was a nasty combination.

"I never mix my drinks." She carefully gave it to him and sat next to him. She leaned over and sucked his lips with a wet kiss.

"I love you." She said.

"I love you too." Kalargo responded.

"What are you watching?" she reached for the remote.

"Nothing really, you can change it if you want" he told her with his plate on his lap just behind his knees.

In the past couple of months their relationship had grown to a more serious than a physical attraction. They bonded so well until they knew mentally that they were meant for each other. But at times she felt like he was too busy for her with work, travel, and the fitness spa. He never thought he was ready to settle down for something as serious as this. He never pressured her in to bed and gave her the utmost respect. At one point she thought he was gay because he had held out for so long. She was convinced, all that had changed when she was allowed to spend the night. For all the time she had waited was so worth that one night of a Jacuzzi bath filled with French vanilla milk and rose peddles floating all around them. The lit candles dripped and filled the bathroom with a cotton candy smell. He picked her up in his arms and let the milk drip dry with rose peddles sticking to her wet body. She knew she would never receive treatment like this from anyone remotely close. He had her when he first poured warm milk on the back of her neck, chest, and hair. The red and white colors were mind blowing; she knew that he knew how to treat a woman to the fullest.

He took his plate in to the kitchen "You know what today's date is?"

"I think it's the twenty second of Dec." She responded.

"Do you have to work tomorrow?" he asked.

"Why?" she asked.

"I just wanted to know if you wanted to work out anytime soon." The faucet water can be heard as he put his plate in the sink.

"Matter of fact, I need to start getting ready, order the rental trucks, oh yeah let me double check on Bennett." He walked in to the bedroom to change clothes.

"Knowing him he went back to sleep..." He thought about it and put the phone down, "...actually, he's pretty reliable." He mumbled to himself.

Due to short notice he was only able to rent six trucks and they had to be picked up by seven pm.

"Jamie, I might have to leave early. What are your plans?"

She walked out of the bathroom flossing her teeth and talking at the same time.
"I should be ready…" She pulled the floss through her back molars "…as soon as I wash up."

He walked across a gray Persian rug as he entered his office and tapped on the key board of his computer to secure the perimeter of his home at three pm. He stood up and retrieved a hand full of fish food from the shelf behind him to feed his piranhas that looked hungry.

His office looked like a corporate space but the size of a bedroom. The thick glass table that held his computer was neatly organized. The blue light in the fish tank exposed the coral reef that he handpicked from Central America. The two marble chiseled tribesman that stood 5 feet with spears and a shield in their hands with twenty-four karat gold eyes. He walked over to his safe and dabbled with the keypad. It beeped and opened on its own.

"Ok, three clips." He grabbed his custom made Chinese Mauser chrome .45 caliber nickel plated, pearl handle with gold screws and aim sight that he got from his dad as a gift. It was engraved, "Life or Death, You choose." It was last produced in the 1920's or 1930's, the Chinese markings on the side meant "Type One". He shoved it in his shoulder holster and slid his arms through. Before he walked out he activated the security alarm.

"Are you ready?" He yelled as he threw on his windbreaker to hide his armor. When he looked into the room she was sliding into her pink thongs with purple butterfly prints. He went to the car. She came out and kissed him on the cheek.

"Hey call me later." They closed their doors and drove off.

The overcast had passed making the sky partly cloudy with slight wind from the east off the beautiful glittering ocean. He could see cargo ships out on the horizon and he knew one of them was a cargo ship named "RUSH". He looked at his car clock and notice that traffic wasn't heavy as usual. For it to be two forty five, that was good he thought, less time he'll have to deal with stupid drivers. His thoughts were interrupted by his cellular.

"Bennett, I knew I could count on you."

"Don't do your counting yet, I was only able to get four men." he can hear Kalargo spitting up cuss words in Korean that he couldn't understand.

"Where is everyone?" he vehemently asked

"Two guys are on the big island and…"

Kalargo's vehemence would have blown a radiator cap, "Bennett! " He paused to calm down. He let out a sigh from deep down.

"Beeeenneeet, listen. Do whatever you need to do to bring the original crew together. Or else tonight will be a long night." He paused to make a right turn to get on the Queen Liliuokalani freeway.

"Have four of the guys meet at your place at five o'clock. I'm on my way, should be there in forty-five minutes. That way we could have the trucks in position." They both agreed and ended the phone call.

Chapter 4

Waikiki beach was crowded with tourist trying to get the ultimate super tan. On a partly cloudy day with showers that had just passed would not stop them from waiting on the beach for the sun to come out. Kalargo drove down Kalakaua Ave and pulled into Kuhio Beach Park parking meter on the beachfront. He sat there just watching the kids play in the sand, and diving off the concrete wall into the waves that rushed the shoreline. He noticed the different cultures that walked and tanned on the beach. A gay couple passed his car holding hands. The volleyball was being chased and kept above ground. Through all of this was like watching a silent scream movie from the interior of his car. He realized that he pulled into the parking lot to get a burger from Jack in the Box. Suddenly he opened his door and beach life was in full swing.

He returned to his car from Kapahulu Ave with a

combo meal. He noticed how dirty his car was. He opened the car door and sat his food on the passenger seat. It was this moment he thought about a friend of his that was killed fifteen years ago in Seoul, South Korea.

On a cold night with snow flurries falling like ash from a distant fire. He was on his way to meet Yhong, a nice fellow, bright and handsome dark tanned Korean. He was supposed to deliver documents that were classified. He found him shot in the head and one bullet in the chest. Did he betray Na Min? Did the Chinese kill him? All these unanswered questions routinely tip toed back into his mind. It was something Yhong wanted to tell him. But by the time he reached him his lungs were drowning him in his own blood. There was nothing he could do but run and avoid questioning. If he had not have been late. He could have helped him, or got a bullet.

By the time he reached Mugumbi's house he was nervous and paced around trying to explain. "Yhong is dead!" he sat down with his palms shielding his face.

He could remember how limp his body was, he was trying to tell him something before he pulled and tugged with his bloody hands on his gray and white button down shirt. He died with Kalargo's ear to his lips.

Mugumbi had just walked in to the house thirty minutes before he did. He was not surprised of this news. Did he know about this already? Kalargo did not know what kind of work he was doing for Na Min so he would have not suspected his own uncle to be the killer.

Mugumbi's first executive party put ten thousand U.S. dollars in his hands. It was his secret between him and Na Min. He was a tall Gambian with a three-inch Afro, faded on the side, with deep sunken eyes that looked like he was on a hunger strike. His lips were a distinctive and very much African that was under a neatly trimmed thick mustache. He always maintained a successful appearance that hid his addiction to heroin.

The drug relaxed him as he listened to Kalargo and thought about his first executive party. The mood, weather, atmosphere, location and the face that he had never forgotten, he was so nervous and scared. The key to the judge's house, and the security code was in Mugumbi's possession. The family was on vacation and he stood in all black in his closet of the master bedroom suite. He remembered the small bubbles of sweat that slowly rolled one by one down the curved valley that followed his spine of his back. The masked that revealed the blood shot red eyes that gave death no chance to run or hide. The heavy steal revolver that was heavier with a silencer. His hands shook and the feeling of moving earthworms crawled on the bottom of his stomach.

The sound of the brakes came to a halt when the judge pulled in front of his house. He took a deep breath, gripped his revolver and tightens the silencer. He held the weapon three inches in front of his face. He held a picture of the judge in his left hand and waited.

Suddenly, Mugumbi had realized his day dream was over and was back in the kitchen, listening to Kalargo babble on about Yhong.

"I can't believe someone would want to kill him." Mugumbi said to comfort him.

Mugumbi's drug addiction started two months after the death of the judge. His now wife Yuki a beautiful exotic Asian lured him in with love and a habit that paid a price. The drug helped him cope with his feelings. The two things he had never forgotten, his first kill and first hit of heroin.

She came in from getting her daily dosage of heroin. The sound of church bells can be heard on this Sunday afternoon under a blue sky with warm intentions. He had wished like hell he could shoot who ever pulling the damn rope to that bell. The traffic of churchgoers passed slowly.

Yuki was no more than 5'5, hundred fifteen pounds, and pale complexion with the most gorgeous eyes. She desired for a bigger rack on her chest, but her buttocks compensated her for that. Her denim jeans, two inch heels and blue leather double breasted coat that was knotted with her belt. Her new hair cut gave her a younger look.

"Hey baby…" he said as she walked in the room. She put her purse on the bed. "How are you feeling?" she asked him. She kicked off her heels and pushed them under the foot of the bed.

"Did you come back with…" she interrupted him. "Are you sure you want to try this?" she held the small baggy in between her right thumb and index fingers. He put his hands on top of hers.

"Yuki…" he paused. "If… it helps me to forget my past and my pain. If it numbs me and makes me feel good like you say it does…" he nodded his head. "I got to have it."

He never told her the real reason just some made up tale about The Gambian police beatings, hangings of his family and friends that haunted him. She also would have never guessed that he was a hit man. He was good at keeping her out of his business.

"Now my love…" she spoke with a syringe horizontally between her lips. She wrapped the belt around his right arm just above his elbow and tightens it to expose his veins. She was teary eyed as a falling tear landed on

63

the crease of his inner elbow; it was like hot acid that boiled into his dark black skin. It slowly made its way down and crossed his up rooted like veins. She sighed as she pulled the cap off the syringe and squirted a little. She used her forearm to wipe her runny eyes to clear her vision for a better aim. She wanted to explain what he should expect but she was interrupted.

"Please, just do it." He begged to get it over with as the needle pinched his skin. His blood mixed with the heroin in the syringe. When she pulled the handle to make sure she had a vein. Then she slowly and carefully pushed the handle of the syringe to insert the brownish liquid monster that will love, neglect, disappoint, numb, and embrace him like no other. His marriage and love affair will be a rocky boundless one that will only give him a temporary escape and a dream that he will only make him more vulnerable.

He realized that he had drifted into a day dream and Kalargo was standing over the kitchen sink trying to clean his shirt of Yhong's blood.

"Uncle, what do you think is going on?"

*   *   *

Honolulu Beach
Back at the beach

The sound of kids passed Kalargo's car as he chewed on a cold French fry with his half empty cup. All this was going through his mind while sitting at the beach. He tossed a French fry in his mouth and took a good chunky bite of his burger.

He wondered what his uncle was up to these days. He picked up his cellular phone and licked his fingers of ketchup and dialed a number.

"Hello Bennett, are you ready? Do you have everything?" he asked. He replied with an assuring voice.

"Of course, we are waiting on you." Bennett said.

He cranks his car. "Ok I'm on my way." And ended the call, he opened his door and tossed the remaining food towards the trash can and missed. He rushed to meet Bennett.

He entered Bennett's house and was immediately approached by him, "Listen, I was only able to round up six trucks. It may take awhile but we'll get it done on time."

Moments later they were on their way to the warehouse.

Kalargo opened the last rusty metal door. "Yes…" he walked over to a stock pile of wooden crates. He repositioned his holster inside his jacket. He stood over a crate that he was about to open. The sound of forklifts and motors revved up, and the loading had begun.

"Ok let me see what I'm sending to my homeland?" he pulled out a RPG-7. The crate contained ten of them. The forklifts continued to load the other crates. In total the shipment manifested Mauser C96's, assault rifles(AK's), light machineguns RPK's and RPD's), M-37's,M-38's, anti armor(RPG-16's), B-10's, M-42's, F-1 anti personnel hand grenades, DS-39's, SG-43 Godunov's, AVS-36's, M1911A1's, Russian M1938's, PPSH41's, DP Ruchnoy Pulemyot light machine guns, RG-42 grenades, and Nambu pistols type 14.

He rolled up his manifest list and tucked it in his back pocket and jumped on a forklift to help loaded the crates.

His cellular rung as he maneuvered the forklift, "Hello."

"Hey what's going on?" the voice sounded familiar. He looked at the screen and realized that it was a Philippine country code. It had to be Jenko.

"Hey where were you? I was just in the Philippines, I tried to get a hold of you." He was excited to hear from his childhood friend.

"I changed my number not long ago. I've been so busy with my new business, man it's crazy. But I finally settled in and this is my new number." Jenko said.

"Jenko…"

"Yeah?" Jenko said.

"I am so in the middle of something." He put the phone down and yelled at his workers, "Come on people, let's stay on schedule." He returned to his conversation. "Are you going to be up later?" Kalargo asked.

"Hey finish what you're doing and give me a call. Any time, Oh before I forget, you think you'll be able to come here for the martial arts competition in July?"

"Wow now that is a good question…" he stopped the forklift to wait to load the next load. He leaned on the wheel, "…I can't really say. I have not missed one yet, but if I can't I will give you a call. Hey, keep in touch and stop being a stranger." The line was dead after they said their goodbyes.

The two of them had been friends since teenagers. They competed against each other in martial arts and Jenko felt second to him to this very day.

"Hey Bennett, how many crates are left to be loaded?" He climbed down from the forklift and pulled himself up on the truck to tie down the cargo.

"Thirty more, we should be done in fifteen minutes."

"Ok listen, meet me at the dock. I'll take three drivers with me so I can start unloading on the ship. The RUSH is at pier 89." He looked at his watch.

"I need three of you to drive!" he yelled over Bennett's shoulder.

"I'll see you there in no more than thirty minutes." He quickly walked away and returned to his supervisory mode.

He pulled out his cellular and noticed that he had four missed calls from Jamie. He decided not to call.

Then he noticed a missed call from Na Min.

"Good morning…" he always spoke to him in Korean to keep him in practice. "How is it going, on schedule?"

"Of course, the first three trucks are on the way. I'm in the first truck."

"I'll call Tomzach." They both ended the line.

*   *   *

The shipping docks were quiet with an occasional ships horn that echoed through the harbor of darkness. The thick fog draped the bay like wet curtains that allowed the low flying screaming seagulls that flew over the choppy water searching for floating trash. The smell of matured exposed fruit with a mixture of caged animals lingered.

Among the ships are two cruise ships that frequently traveled from Waikiki to Los Angeles and three super cargo ships down there was a small beat up two hundred yard rust can known as the "RUSH".

Captain Tomzach peered through his binoculars. He stood in a crimson trench coat with a white lapel and gold metallic buttons with two huge anchors on both sides. He was 5'11, 230 lbs Russian that spoke fluent Korean and horrible English. He looked like a fifty year old who just graduated from boot camp.

His Russian accent rolled off his tongue.

"Get that crane ready and put this load aft of the ship on the starboard."

"Yes, they are on time." He said and looked down at his wrist watch. He picked up the ship's phone to inform his crew to prepare for loading.

Kalargo stepped out of the truck before it came to a complete stop. He directed the following trucks to wait in line. He waved to Captain Tomzach and approached the ramp of the ship.

"Welcome aboard." The captain greeted him with a firm hand shake.

"Is everything going accordingly?"

He sighed, "As planned, are they ready to load them?"

The captain held up his left index finger, "My men are always ready."

He looked him in his eyes. He picked up the ships phone and gave a command in horrible English to start loading.

After two hours, the eastern morning sky commenced to brighten and the herd of ship yard employees slowly dragged their feet like they were forced to go to a funeral.

Kalargo's crew had finished just in time before shift changed and he stopped by the security gate to drop off a brown paper bag to the guard. They shook hands as the last truck passed. "Now you don't spend all that in one place."

"Oh don't worry Mr. Choi, I have a special place for it." He smiled and tucked it away in behind his security belt until he got home.

Chapter 5

Gambia, West Africa

The African country of the Gambia is located on the northern west coast of Africa and bordered Senegal. For many years it was not known for having any significant natural resources. Seventy percent depends on crop and live stock for its livelihood. A small-scale manufacturing activity features the process of peanuts, fish, and hide.

In a small village of Farafenni, Gambia, a Korean team

of prospectors discovered that north of the Gambian river had an abundance of diamonds, gold, and oil. The civil war that lasted for more than twenty five years had prevented the successes and growth. The North Koreans were supplying the rebels with weapons to overthrow King Shabonee with the help of double agent Na Min.

King Shabonee had two wives, three daughters and two sons that died in a genocide blood bath. The village that spoke his native tongue had been burned to the ground, and to make sure that no one could claim the throne. Everyone in the village was beheaded. The rebels gutted the pregnant women like fish to make sure there were no surviving sons.

But the King had one brother that did survive and gave him the position of General of the Gambian army. It would be thirty years later when he would find out that he had one son who escaped the genocide.

The civil war had replaced this beautiful country of green mountains, waterfalls, and culture friendly into a divided population.

Attaining control of this government would bring prosperity to those outside of this country. It's a new frontier that has not been touched. The most fascinating question is who would control these natural resources?

The United Nations has hesitated; neighboring countries has no desire to get involved. The country of Senegal closed their borders to over two hundred fifty thousand refugees that now live along their border. These innocent people are dying by the hundreds. The King ordered all men, women, boys and girls as young as twelve to bear arms. He would not allow the Gambian Islamic republic Army who are being funded with weapons by a communist country to over throw his government.

King Shabonee sat in front of his bedroom window overlooking the city of Gunjur. His beautiful view of the North Atlantic Ocean was breath taking. He held his oxygen mask to his face and fogged it with his breath. He had grown old, ill, but most importantly, still alive. A servant knocked on his door.

"Your majesty…" Paul slowly twisted the knob and peeked in. "…I hope I am not disturbing you, do you mind?"

The King looked over his shoulder and twisted himself to see him. "Paul?"

"Yes, it is me."

The King turned to his view watching the small fishermen coming in from the Ocean. He put his oxygen mask on his lap. "Come on in Paul, how is your day?"

Paul entered humbled with his hands along his side. "I have good news to report, the General has taken control of the northern side of the river. The war is turning in our favor. He is doing an excellent job."

He offered the King a cup of tea, "Morning tea?" he held the empty cup up before he poured the tea.

The King sighed as a relief that he has finally gained control of half of his country. He smiled and rubbed his chin.

"Paul…" The King slowly stood and dragged his green oxygen tank to where he stood.

"Do you need…" before he could ask if he needed help walking. The King had refused.

"I think I will pour my own cup of tea today" he smiled at him and patted him on the shoulder. They celebrated with tea.

*   *   *

Honolulu, Hi

The sun slowly made its way through Kalargo's room. His right eye slowly
opened with eye snot in the corners, lucky his uncle was not around.

"Oh my god," He looked at the clock "damn, three o'clock already." He batted his eyes to adjust his vision. He quickly covered his face in the pillow and grunted. He felt hungry. But stood up, walked and stretched his way towards the bathroom. The phone rang.

"Oh great timing, whoever it is can wait." He mumbled.

A message was not left. "I guess it wasn't that important." A few moments later, it rang again. He leaned over the toilet and urinated. He sighed. After the third, he answered. "Hello."

There was silence for a moment, "Good afternoon." Her voice was erotic as always. "I was trying to get a hold of you last night." She said. Before he could respond, "How would you like to meet a friend of mine? She's coming in from San Diego." She waited for his response.

He paused, "Well…" He tried to quickly think of what he had to do later on that day, "…hmmm, well I don't have anything planned, yeah why not." His face was two inches away from the bathroom mirror softly touching a zit. He frowned.

"I've told her about you…" she was interrupted.

"What time does her flight arrive?"

"She is going to call me when she arrive to her hotel. That should be around four o'clock. I'll call you, how that sounds?"

He sighed with a yawn that followed. "Good, I am just waking up. Make sure you call first." They ended the call.

After a quick shower he splashed his favorite cologne on his abdominal and neck. He noticed the time and wondered how long he can live like this. He picked up his cell phone and dialed a long distance number. He waited patiently for an answer. Finally he terminated the call. He walked into the kitchen, but thought about where his uncle Mugumbi could be. For years he thought his uncle lived a modest life with his girlfriend.

He opened the refrigerator and grabbed a bowl of green seedless grapes, walked over to the French doors that over looked the pool. He thought about his first murder. Though it was in self defense, his true colors came out. He found out that his uncle was a hit man for the North Koreans.

His thought took him back ten years, it was Perth, Australia.
"Do you know these people?!"

"Make a left off the highway exit!" Mugumbi said before he could inquire for more information there were more directions to follow.

It was three o'clock in the morning with patches of fog that creped slowly across the highway from a soiled field along side. The nearest town outside of Perth was miles

away. He drove at speeds up to a hundred twenty miles per hour. Their hearts were pumping like generators. The sweat that soaked their backs was uncomfortable and the last thing they wanted to think about. The rental car fish tailed as they ran a yellow light changed to red. Mugumbi looked back to see if
they were still in chase.

"What is the hell going on?!" he desperately wanted to know. Mugumbi opened the glove compartment and pulled out two desert eagles chrome pistols. He shoved the clips into them both.

"Damn..." He swallowed and sighed

Mugumbi could not, by all means tell him about the assassinations of this list of wealthy and powerful people. They both frequently looked into the mirrors. But Mugumbi sighed, and decided not to tell him.

"Make a left!"

"Ok, I'll tell you, but you can't tell anybody. I mean, not a sole." He hesitated and looked back and noticed the head lights right on their tail. Damn near kissing their bumper, "I am a hit man."

"What! Get out of here!"

"Listen earlier I just killed a man. That's what I do. I kill for a living. Now take this gun, because tonight will be your first kill, so man up." He handed the pistol to him with the handle in his hand. He grabbed it by the handle and looked in the rear view mirror.

"Make a right! Make a right!" he told him. The sound of gun fire erupted, but the early morning dew had dampened the road. The car lost control and hit a ditch. It did not take long before all hell broke loose. The car landed in a muddy cow pasture.

"We got to get out of here, now! Let's go!" Mugumbi took the lead, despite the minor injuries; he grabbed him by the shirt, they made their way across the field to a barn. Kalargo was scared and he felt his legs weaken as he ran for his life. The ankle deep mud slowed them but they used the cows as cover until they got to the barn.

"Hey stand here, I'll be over there. When I start shooting, I want you to hold your fire until I whistle. Then you let them have it." He walked away to the other side of the barn.

Kalargo stood in between a group of cows. He still remembered that stench and how his shoes were ruined. He remembered the cold chrome barrel that he rubbed against his forehead. How his hands shook because his mind told him he was going to die in a barn with cow shit on his damn shoes, before he could say a prayer, gun shots were fired from an automatic. The cows began to run. It was now or never. He started shooting after he heard the whistle. He shot two of the guys and Mugumbi shot and killed the other.

Kalargo ran over and kicked the mac-10 away from the hands from one of them. The other guy laid face up gagging and holding his throat. The bullet went through his neck. He stood there in shock.

"Well, what are you waiting on?"

The other survivor looked up at them with a bullet in his upper torso. The full moon lit the cloudless sky and provided enough light to see the eyes of this older man.

"Well, it's your kill. You shot him. You finish him."

Mugumbi walked over to the guy he shot and put another bullet in his head.

Kalargo looked at him.

"Well, I thought I heard him breathe..." He frowned at him, "...just a little bit." His accent was stronger than his because he learned English later in life.

Mugumbi walked over to him and stood behind him. "Listen..." he held Kalargo's arm up and aimed the pistol. "...Just." He spoke with a calm and relaxed voice, "...aim, and just pulled the trigger. Trust me, the last thing you need is to see this ass hole again one day." He whispered in his ear. He looked at his uncle and sighed. He quickly pulled the trigger four times. His nerves in his stomach were jumping like they were attached to a jack hammer.

He patted him on his back, "Welcome to a world that not many people have a chance to experience. Hey, it was self-defense. You can always tell your innersoul that, if that'll make you comfortable, at least I won't tell anyone."

He looked at his uncle, and shoved the pistol into his gut.

"Look at it this way; you never have to kill him twice."

" Now I can live with that" Kalargo told him.

He thought to himself, "Ten years went fast." The taste of a bad grape reminded him that he was in his living room overlooking the pool through the French doors.

*   *   *

Later that evening

"Hello." Kalargo spoke into his cellular.

Jamie spoke over the music in the background. "Are you busy?"

"Of course not…" Kalargo said.

"We are going out to dinner at Nicholis Nicholis. Do you think you can meet us there?" Jamie asked.

He was looking through his closet. "Sure I can. What time?"

"Ten thirty, I made reservations already. We'll see you there." They ended the call.

He entered his office and called Na Min. He sat at his desk with his feet propped on the edge of the two-inch thick glass.

"Annyong-haseyo…" Kalargo said.

Na Min was happy to hear from him, "Kalargo, I've been expecting your call. I've already transferred those funds. How did last night go? No problems?"

Kalargo slightly twisted his neck and spoke with confidence. "Of course not, you know how those last minute decisions are handled."

They both grinned a little. "How's Jamie doing?"

"Just fine, matter of fact her and I are meeting tonight for dinner."

"She's a beautiful woman. I can see you and her being together for a very long time…" he quickly changed the subject, "…when was the last time you spoke to your uncle?"

He was surprised to be asked. "Actually I tried to call him today. But I got the answering machine."

"Have you heard about the store they opened?"

"What! He didn't tell me about that. That son of a gun, he's moving up in the world." He sighed.

"So that's the second store. The first one is in Osan. Where is the…" before he could finish.

"Yes, and the other store is in Pusan. Him and his wife…" he was interrupted.

"What, he tied the knot? After all these years…" he rubbed his left index finger across his eyebrow, "…he could have invited me." He sighed.

"Hey I don't mean to be rude but I'm a little busy. However I wanted to tell you about the transfer, and to keep up the good work." Before he could end the call Kalargo asked him about the civil war in The Gambia.

"Everything's going accordingly, sometime this week we'll have to sit down
and discuss an important issue." he spoke with a more serious tone.

"If you are flying in from South Korea, it has to be important." He told him.

"Anyway, I'll give you a call. Until then, make sure you call your uncle." He agreed and they ended the call.

Kalargo flipped the switch on the computer and within minutes he was looking at his bank account. He transferred the funds to his business account, "Southern Pacific Martial Arts and Fitness" and most to a Swiss account. He smiled at the screen and decided to give his employees a bonus.

Moments later, the phone rang. "Hello."

The voice on the other end sounded muffled and echoed. "Hey Kalargo…"

"Yeah, who is this?" Kalargo said.

He looked down at the caller id and did not recognize the area code or country code. "This is Crockett!"

"Heeey Crockett. Long times no hear, what's going on?" Kalargo asked, before he could respond, "Where are you?"

He barely understood him. "I just arrived in Bahrain, a small island in the Persian Gulf."

"Wow that big ship pulled into port?"

Crockett wiped his forehead of sweat. "No actually we flew in from the carrier."

Kalargo leaned back and relaxed. "It's kind of hectic over in the Persian Gulf with Sadam acting a fool. You boys will be at war soon. What is it called, Desert Storm?"

"Yep, but I'm lucky I'll be in Bahrain, fifty miles from Saudi Arabia and three hundred miles from Kuwait." He stood in a small red phone booth.

"I know you wish you were back in Hawaii or at the least the Philippines?"

Kalargo asked. "You have no idea how long you'll be over there?"

"It's no telling, may be six months."

"Well…" he was interrupted.

"I might see you when I pass through for the martial arts competition in the Philippines."

"Well I'm not sure if I will fly back or go back by ship. I would hate to miss a port of call in Australia." The phone booth was like a lava pit. "I've been here five days and haven't seen a woman yet. They are all wrapped up"

They both laughed. "Hey be happy you're not in Afghanistan where they are covered from head to toe, and if caught starring to long is considered stalking." They laughed hard.

"Well I am guilty as hell. Listen I have to go, I am running out of minutes." he quickly said. "When I get out I was thinking about working for you. You know once I get out of the military. It's time to make some real money. But we…" The female voice interrupted his conversation to advise him of his remaining seconds.

"Hey, you just keep your head low. The most important thing is making it back. I'll always have a place for you ok, but next time call me collect." They both agreed and ended the call.

Chapter 6

Kalargo grabbed his keys and walked out the door. He wore a black Giovanni Versace suit with a white button up shirt. He looked his Lexus over for dirt. He sat in the driver seat and pushed the number three for his theme song, "Pay Back" by James Brown. He looked in the rear view mirror to make sure his face was clear of shameful objects. He opened the arm rest and lifted a bottle of Available by All Means cologne. He turned up the music and drove to the Nicholis Nicholis.

It was a Tuesday night with a slight breeze from the east with clear skies. He arrived at the hotel that hosted the restaurant on the thirty-second floor.

He pulled up to valet and the attendant gave him a ticket, exited and casually walked into the hotel. Before he could push the button, a couple entered the elevator, obviously drunk and having a good time.

"What floor?"

"Fifteen please." She said.

Her breast was literally falling out of her non-supportive dress. He looked away and pushed fifteen on the panel.

"Sorry." The female said as they stumbled out on the fifteenth floor. Her dark brunette hair with a small amount of gray strings gave her a Spanish look. He guessed that she had to be at least forty-five. Her earrings were studded with diamonds that matched her bracelet. He sighed with a smile and pushed the button.

He rubbed his mustache and eyebrows as he looked in the elevator mirror. As each floor passed the sound of the bell would ding, twenty-one, twenty two, and etc.

Finally, the elevator opened on the thirty-second floor and the skyline of Waikiki was beautiful. The live band can be heard. The candles that lit each table gave a welcoming feeling.

The host welcomed him. "Mr. Choi, your party awaits you. How is everything?"

He was known here like it was a second home, "Just fine and you Steve?"

Jamie walked over and gave him hug and a kiss.

"We have a table by the window" she told him as they approached this white and burgundy clothed table.

Her friend was a gorgeous knock out blonde. She stood and greeted him. The waiter spoke to him, "I just started my shift. You enjoy. Your waiter will be with you shortly, drinks?"

He pulled his seat out and slowly sat down. "Give me a wine cooler, with the lemon flavor."

"Ladies and you're having?" Steve asked.

"I'll have a glass of your house wine." Jamie ordered, Stacy requested the same.

"So, this is Stacy the world has been talking about." He reached over to shake her hand, "...and I am Kalargo. I hope Jamie has told you all the good things about me." He smiled; his African accent can be heard a little on certain words.

"I've heard so much about you." She said.

He grunted, "I'm an ok type of guy."

She leaned forward. Her long hair was pinned up in a bun, but a small portion was in her face, using her thumbs to separate and push it behind her ears. Her lips were lined with a pencil. She was like a Barbie that had walked out of the Barbie doll factory. Her deep cleavage allowed her breast to rest on the table, not that he was starring, but, hey they were actually starting to talk to him.

"I…" She paused.

"And here are your drinks." The waiter placed them on the table, "Would you like to order or you need more time?"

They looked at each other and agreed for more time. The waiter quickly walked away.

"Listen she was trying to tell me how you, how can I say it. Came here from Africa, is it true?" she looked him in his eyes.

Jamie interrupted, "Girl he doesn't want to talk about that stuff. Those were painful memories."

"Were they? I mean if you choose not to talk about it I would totally understand." Stacy said with a humbled voice.

He leaned forward and held Jamie's hand, "Well…" He looked

her in the eyes. "There is something that I have not told anyone." He sighed and swallowed air.

"I tell you what. Lets order and then I'll tell you how I and my uncle made our journey." He said as he looked over the menu. They agreed.

Stacy had to be no more than 5'8, hundred thirty five pounds, straight blonde hair that came to the middle of her back, thirty eight double d and her lips were glossy, and kissable. She wore a satin dress that came two inches above her knees. Her tan was perfect. All of Stacy's gestures said to come home with me, not next week, or next month but right now.

"Is this your first time in Hawaii?" Kalargo looked at Stacy.

"Yes, she has been trying to have me visit her for years." She looked out of the huge picture window at the sky line. "It's so beautiful and scenic. I should have come a long time ago." She sighed.

"Girl, it took this long to get you here, now I hope it won't take the same amount of time to convince you to stay." Jamie grabbed her hand and they both smiled.

He thought that they were mighty touchy and clingy, but that's how females are in America he told himself.

"What do you think about her staying in Hawaii?" Jamie asked him.

He had to quickly pull his tongue out of Stacy's panties. He frowned. "Why not… I." He paused. "I'll leave it up to you guys. It is kind of expensive to live here." He sighed. "But…" He frowned and touched his mustache. "…I 'm sure she'll find work…" He was interrupted.

The waiter accosted the table. "Hello…" He stood with his hands behind his back. "Are you guys ready to order yet?" He asked with a patient but feminine voice and gesture.

Kalargo rubbed his stomach.

"Hmm, yes I would say we are ready. I'll have whatever the special is." He looked at them to confirm.

They ordered their food while he patiently wrote everything down. He repeated their order and asked. "Anything else you would like to add?"

They were sure they had everything. He sighed and closed his eyes, rubbed the back of his neck. He took a swallow of his wine. Jamie and Stacy waited for this amazing story of survival.

"Ok, Africa, well I was born in a small village and from my understanding. My whole family was killed. The village was burned to the ground. My uncle took me from The Gambia, Africa to South Africa and worked in a diamond mine. He was later laid off and found work at the port loading cargo."

Thinking of these events had his eyes pinkish red, tearful and increased his heart beat. He sighed and continued.

"Well…" He decided to skip a portion; "It was so many years ago, I had to be, what, nine?" He put his hands together in front of his face, rested his chin between his thumb and the bottom of his index finger. He told an intriguing story.

It was the early 70's

"Kalargo, you see that crate…" Mugumbi asked, "…You have to get inside, it's the only way we can go to America."

"I stood on the pier behind six foot crates stacked on top of each other. A small amount of people working at three o'clock in the morning but the crowd had not arrived." He swallowed a good portion of his wine to remove the itchy sand paper feeling that lay at the bottom of his throat.

"I'm scared." I told him, "He grabbed me by my shirt and yanked me towards him." He paused.

"You listen to me. This is not the time to be scared! This is our only chance to get out of here!" He spoke with passion. His gestures were almost vivid. His hands were in front of him just as if he had taken the place of his uncle.

"If we get caught trying to go away as stowaway. We will regret it for the rest of our lives!" Mugumbi's hard whisper vibrated his ears.

"For six months I've been planning this trip. There is no time to horse around. Now crawl in!" He demanded.

He gently placed his hands on the table. Stacy and Jamie were totally blown away. The music by the band was tuned out. He had them by their ears like kids that were in trouble. Their eyes were fixed on his lips. He took a moment to look them in their wet eyes. He had noticed that they both were in shock and scared for his ordeal, but could not wait for what would happen next.

"Duck down! Shhh…" They quickly hid behind a wall of crates. A worker walked by, "Listen Tipi, These crates are next to be loaded, we have to do this now!" The look on Mugumbi's face was like the eyes of a lion, a mad pissed off lion.

"I crawled in and he told me, now listen, whatever you do. Don't panic! You see these holes. Use them for breathing. I will come looking for you in four hours. He knew the order of loading. My crate will be on top. I'll come and get you out." He told me.

He gave me my travel bag that had food. He closed the crate. It was dark and scary. The heat was unbearable. The stench made me vomit so much I gave up on trying to hold it in. I was in this motionless position that had paralyzed me."

"I cried when I felt the crane lift the crate into the air. I felt like a caged animal. I held on to my bag and closed my eyes. For the first time I told God that I was scared and I asked him to watch over me. I went to sleep."

Jamie and Stacy were so into his story. They forgot all about their drinks.

"I mean, of course I trusted him with my life, besides he did most of the loading on the pier. So I had no reason not to believe what he was telling me." He rubbed his face with his hands and shook his head. He scratched the back of his neck and leaned back into the chair. He was exhausted. The story brought back memories; the kind that would make a kid wet his pants.

His voice was lowered. "It, we were in those crates for three days!" He whispered like a kitten. He held his hands together in a praying form. His humbled voice could reach out and touch any ones heart. He sighed.

"I was sea sick two different times. The Indian Ocean

truly has no mercy on a weak stomach." He rubbed his stomach.

"I heard a voice calling me. Tipi, are you OK?" I was weak. My lips were dry, too weak to respond, my uncle opened the crate. He threw water on my face. I was so thirsty; I tried to lick my forehead." He smiled but he was serious. "I almost died. He lifted my hand, and told me we made it. We are here." He told me. He gave me some food that he had gotten out of the garbage. Damn it was good to have something, anything. I can't tell you what it was. It was all mixed up with other food that was tossed out. But I know it was fresh, because it warmed my palms as I ate it out of my hands." He folded his lips inward and continued his story.

"When the ship docked in South Korea..." their eyes and mouth open wider, "... yes, I said South Korea." He gasped for air and the girls swallowed his pain.

"Because my uncle couldn't read, he assumed that the ship was going to America..." He leaned forward and looked them directly in their eyes, "...and we damn sure didn't speak Korean!"

"What the hell happened?" Somehow Stacy asked without moving her lips.

"Well the ship had an American flag on it, but it went to..." He had this look of surprise. "South Korea."

Their mouths were literally on the table. "No way!" they looked at each other.

"My legs were numb. I was wet from urine and defecation. The smell of just me was enough to commit suicide. I was out of food after my third day. As far as being thirsty, I drank whatever I had to drink, and yes my

88

own urine." He frowned, "Somehow my uncle thought it took four days to get to America." He laughed.

They both slithered their tongues out in disgust. Jamie wiped her eyes with the back of her hand. She carefully tried not to smear her makeup.

"I couldn't do it…" Stacy said.

He interrupted her. "Trust me; never say what you won't do." He waved his left index finger in front of them.

"I thank God my uncle made me drink water for three days straight before our trip. I just can't imagine…" He paused. He was going to continue but the waiter had delivered their food.

"OK, you ordered the house special, all three of you. " His female like voice was distinctive. He also thought Kalargo was handsome. He placed the plates on the table. The steam from the food can be seen.

Jamie looked at her plate and said, "Excuse me, hmm. What in the world is this?" She looked cute and timid as her curiosity gave suspicion. The waiter smiled and batted his lightly lined eyes.

"That is squid covered with a lightly marinated peanut butter, a splash of lemon, and on the side. You have garlic bread and pasta with a squid sauce that's buttered." He stood with his hands behind his back.

"Have you tried this? "Stacy asked him.

"No, but I heard it's good and very healthy." He paused. "If you have found it not what you want, I'll be more than happy to replace it. No problem." They agreed.

Kalargo quickly mixed his squid into his pasta and commenced to chow down on his food. "Now this is good."

He added more seasoning and squeezed a tab bit of lemon, with his mouth filled to his gills, he said, "I remember the first time I had this." He used the table napkin to wipe his lips. "I had to be… what ten years old. It's a Korean dish that is usually served as a celebration, but now a day, it's more or less a regular meal."

He held the fork in his right hand and pointed it at their plate. "But, you do have to acquire a taste for it." He smiled.

It was at this moment Stacy was overwhelmed by this burning desire to have sex with him. She liked how his broken English rolled off his lips, and how intelligent he is. He knew so much about other places. He was so intriguing. Her eyes were wet, but her panties were wetter, she cried and wiped her eyes. She knew it would never happen. He just didn't seem like that type of guy, someone that would understand her.

At the end of their dinner they rubbed their bellies and declared themselves full.

"Not bad, for a plate of, whatever it was." She smiled and pushed her plate away. Stacy looked at Jamie.

"You still wanted to see his house?" she asked her, before she could respond he raised his hand like a child in grade school that had an answer to a question,

"Check please. Oh yeah, you wanted to see my house? It's OK." He said as he pushed his shoulders up.

"I have to return for something anyway." He thought

about her and how she's been playing footsy under the table with him.

In his mind he had to ask himself 'what kind of a friend is she? She just met me and flirting with me?' He thought all of it was strange.

Later, they arrived at his house, the touch of a button, his double iron gates opened. Stacy's eyes open wide.

"Wow…" she looked out the window like a kid's first time at Disney World and all the cartoon characters were lined to meet her.

This is gorgeous and wondered how he can afford such a luxurious place.
Like a tour guide, Jamie explained the designs and culture behind the architecture.

"As you can see how fond he is of the Oriental culture…" she pointed out the native plants from South Korea, arches, and Buddha.

"Now whatever you do…" they closed the doors to the car. "Don't step on his rose garden." Stacy carefully made sure not to.

After showing Stacy around Jamie pulled him into the bathroom.

"I know what you are thinking and she's not your type." She smiled as she unzipped his pants and pulled out his penis. He chuckled and looked directly in her eyes. His thumb slowly and lightly touched her forehead. She sat on the toilet and put his python in her mouth.

Suddenly, there was a knock at the door. "Jamie, where is the T.V. and entertainment you told me about, from behind the door his soft voice said, "She's busy. But the remote that's on the coffee table, push the second red, button." A brief pause before he could catch his breath. He combed his fingers through her hair, "Yeah, just push the red button and aim it at the wall across from the couch.

Stacy put her ear to the bathroom door, giggled with her hands over her mouth and tiptoed away. The red button produced an entertainment center from the floor and she was entertained.

Moments later, Jamie entered the living room with a smile, "Girl..." Stacy put her hands over her mouth. "Shhh... I don't want to hear it." They both laughed.

"Jamie, where did you find this man?" Stacy looked at her with this curious look. Her lips tooted up as she tilted her head.

Jamie flopped on to the couch, crossed her legs and signed.

"You could have at least tried to brush your hair and wiped a little lipstick on or something." They both giggled like teens. Stacy leaned over, "What does he do?" She asked with curiosity.

The phone rang. "Do you want me to get that?" Jamie asked.

Kalargo's voice came from behind the bedroom door. "I got it! Hello."

The voice on the receiver was deep and troubled.

"Kalargo, the warehouse was raided!" Bennett said.

"What! Who all was arrested?" Kalargo asked.

He sounded like he was almost out of breath. "Pat, Damion, and big Mike. I had just left and I'll be damn…" He paused.

"Do you know who raided?"

"Honolulu police, it looked like they were looking for drugs. You need to call the dock!" He said.

"Who is the weakest link of them all?"

Bennett paused, "Damion."

"Well, get the lawyer and bail them all out, make sure you bail Damion out first. Was anything left behind?"

"No."

"But if they interrogate Damion long enough. They might find out that it's on the dock and the answer to your question, everything was already taken to the dock."

"I'll call you back. I got to call the dock." The phone call ended.

He slammed his fist down on the desk, "Shit." He dialed captain Tomzack's number nervously.

After the phone call he sat on the edge of the desk with his head in his palms. His buzz from the alcohol slowly drifted away. He heard the music coming from the living room. He thought of Stacy tits and ass.

"Hey." He rose up and threw on a pair of jeans. He applied green apple lotion and a small amount of Hugo

Boss cologne on his chocolicious body.

"Sorry for being a horrible host." He walked out bare footed. Stacy legs were slightly open.

"Jamie, you didn't offer her anything?"

"We were just sitting here thumbing through the music and talking about old times."

He walked over to the wet bar. "Let me see… I have Cognac, white wine or Vodka."

Jamie immediately said, "I'll have some white wine. Do you have any strawberries or grapes?"

Stacy boldly requested, "I'll have the bottle of cognac." She let out a strong sigh that lifted her small strands of hair from the front of her face.

He thought if she drinks this bottle, it's over. The freak will for sure come out tonight, he spoke beneath his breathe. I'll have her stripping and eating Jamie's crotch and sucking me like a drunken vacuum." He continued to speak to himself.

"My God, it's going to be a fabulous night and Jamie, she'll be
too drunk to remember anything." He smiled.

"Ladies…" He gave them a glass and begins pouring Jamie's drink first. Stacy quickly grabbed the cognac bottle, popped the cork and slammed the mouth of the bottle like she had deep throated before. His eyes opened wide.

"Oh my…" He looked at Jamie. "You might need to keep an eye on her." He said with a sarcastic voice. He turned up the music and told them he'll be back. He slipped into his office. He sighed and used his palms to push the stress from his eyes to his ears and to the back of his neck.

"I got to call Na Min…" He held the phone in his left hand and sighed.

"This is going to be harder than I thought" He pushed the first number. "If I do it now, I won't be interrupted later."

"Good evening." he answered the phone. They spoke in Korean. He let him know that it was a small matter and it was nothing to worry about. Their conversation ended.

He returned to the living room. "Surprise, I am back." He stopped dead in his tracks. The bottle of cognac that was full was now half full. He pretended like he didn't see it.

"They were laughing from the top of their gills. They had tears rolling down their faces. The wild life channel showed a rare monkey encounters with a female monkey. The Japanese monkeys were in a cage. When the monkeys are having sex, the jealous male monkeys attack the male while he's having sex, knowing that he won't stop having sex until he has an orgasm. They immediately run when they are finish. The zoo doctors said that this is the only time they have an advantage in fighting this male monkey. He flopped down between them and laughed like he had never seen it before. Jamie leaned on him putting her right hand on his stomach. Stacy laughed so hard at the monkeys facial expressions until tears fell. Her legs were open and rubbing against his.

The monkeys yanked on his tail, punched and vigorously pulled his facial hair. He looked so pissed off, but like usual he didn't stop.

Stacy grabbed the bottle of cognac and took a huge gulp. At the same time Jamie looked at him, "Don't pay her any attention."

She held her stomach to reduce the pain that her laughter gave her. She stood and laughed her way to the kitchen, obviously drunk.

"Why is your kitchen moving so much?" She asked.

Jamie looked at him, "Nope... don't think about it."

For some reason no matter how idiotic she looked. She looked hot as hell. Suddenly the phone rang, "Thank God." Jamie said.

After three rings he had not moved, "Go ahead and get the phone... tell them I'm not here."

She picked up the phone, "Hello..." She looked at him. "It sounds very important." She handed him the receiver.

"I'll take it in the office." He grunted like a kid.

Jamie walked over to her, "Why are trying to lead him on?"

Her eyes blood shot red and a fresh smell of cognac on her breath. She slowly and carefully leaned forward. "You told me..." Jamie was interrupted. Stacy softly placed her index over her lips.

"I am just having fun." She held on to Jamie for support.

"I really don't mean any harm." She struggled to return

to the coach. Her words drooled off her lips, "Jamie…" her eyes filled with tears.

"Why can't I find me a man like you?" She slowly shook her head and scratched her neck. Jamie laid her down on the couch.

"No harm intended, you know everyone tell me that I am so beautiful, but I can't keep a man." She reached for the bottle. Jamie pulled her hand.

"No… I think you've had enough of that. Have you spoken to anyone about this?" Jamie asked her.

She looked her in the eyes; she softly bit her bottom lip. "Girl, it's been an ongoing nightmare." She used her left pinky finger to dig into her right ear.

"Did I ever tell you how jealous I was of you? Every since we were kids… I think I was cursed." She pushed her tears back and buried her face into the pillow. Jamie began to emotionally break down. Her best friend in the world is deeply depressed. She gave her a hug. They both burst into tears. She grabbed her hands and brought them to her face. "Stacy, you have to stay strong!"

"I know, but it's so hard!" Stacy whispered. "And one understands." She looked Jamie in her eyes and grunted.

"I am fucked up." She said.

Jamie stopped her. "No, you are my friend. You are Stacy." They both laughed and kissed each other on the lips.

Kalargo came from the room partially dressed, "Ladies… I'll be right back."

Jamie rose from the couch and walked over to him. "Is everything OK?"

"Yeah…"

She looked over her shoulder as she walked him to the door.

"I just have to take care of something. I'll be back." He gave her a passionate kiss on her lips and held her tight.

"I apologize for Stacy." She said.

He wedged his lips between hers and French kissed her. He inhaled her breath with his eyes closed.

"If I ever wanted a best friend, it would be you." He held her hand as he walked to the door. She leaned her head in his upper arm. It was this moment that he had realized how he truly felt for her.

"Put Stacy in the guest room." He opened the door. "When I get back, I want you in your birthday suit." They giggled and kissed each other good-bye.

Chapter 7

Seoul, South Korea

Agent Na Min Choi sat at his desk. His diamond channel set pinky ring sparkled when he reached for the phone. He dialed his step daughter's home and waited for someone to answer. His old fashion reading glasses sat at the lower tip of his nose, his beige robe with gold initials, "NC". It was early in the morning, but this call was important. His step daughter answered in Korean. "Annyong-haseyo"

"Hello Yuki, don't mean to call you so late…" he was interrupted.

"Daddy, I was thinking of you earlier today. How is everything?"

He sighed, "Well…" He never discusses his business with her and she totally understood.

"Let's say a little hectic." He paused like he had a lot on his mind.

"Your work is going to kill you; it's time for you to retire." Her words melted the wax in his ears. "Yeah in another five years."

But she knew he could afford to retire now but he was in too deep. She looked over at Mugumbi, "Well I am sure if you are calling this late, you must be calling for Mugumbi."

She heard his sigh, "I love you my dear."

"Yes I know." She gave the phone to her husband. "Honey, it's my dad."

Na Min tapped the tip of his fingers on the calendar that covered his desk. It was seconds before Mugumbi cleared his throat with his face half buried into the pillow. His Korean was horrible in the morning hours, day hours, and whenever he tried to speak Korean, "Annyong-haseyo."

Whenever he called for business their dialogue was always coded to their understanding. "I am inviting you to the next executive party." His voice was calm.

He looked at the clock, "OK."

"I know this is bad timing, but I need you on the next flight to Hawaii. You will have more details once you get there." He circled a date on his calendar, "Next flight?" He sighed.

"Not a problem." Mugumbi closed his eyes.

A the age of forty seven he felt like a thirty year old, fit, healthy, but his down fall is his addiction. So far it has not yet interfered with his work. He used his left thumb to snatch an annoying nose hair. He looked at it.

"Is everything else OK?" Na Min asked.

"Oh yeah, can't compliant. Listen, I will call you when I touch down on the island." The line ended.

Na Min removed his glasses, grabbed his bottle of Gin and thought about the first time he met Ginifer. He looked at the glass and asked, "I no longer wonder how you have become my best friend?"

Of course she did not respond. He liked that about her. She gave him no lip, no limit to her love, and most of all, she had given him plenty of nights of satisfaction, and someone to talk to. She relieved him of bad dreams of those unspeakable acts to humans for the name of national security. Some times their faces haunted him in his sleep. He knew he could tell her his deepest secrets without her going around blabbing his business and getting him in trouble. He also knew that Ginifer was slowly killing him. His liver was not functioning properly. He picked up his glass of Gin and slowly touched his lips. He kissed edge of the shot glass and licked the rim. It was cold, he tilted it just enough to sip her wetness. She was warm and soaking wet, the no longer burning of his throat made their bond stronger. He looked at the glass.

"Am I an alcoholic, nope? Not I say Ginifer." Na Min grinned.

He twisted the shot glass and poured it in to his mouth like he was doing something super special. His tongue was relieved, his throat burned just enough to remind him of their bond, but not like it used to. Her strength was no longer potent.

"Am I losing my love for her?" He asked himself, "Ginifer?" He tilted his head to the left, raised his voice and looked at the glass and then the bottle.

"Now you know, you and I go way back. We can talk about anything." He tilted his head like she was naughtier than he.

"You are not satisfying me like you used to. Is there anything that you would like to tell me?" He examined the bottle to make sure he had not substituted her for a cheaper whore in a bottle form. He knew she would not have liked that.

"Never." He poured another shot.

Suddenly his wife knocked at the door. "Is everything OK?" She peeked in on him trying to make love to Ginifer. He was caught in the act. She once told him that she was no good for him. He looked at her.

"Just finishing my dear, I'll be to bed soon, just cleansing my breath." He quickly downed Ginifer one last time for the night and tucked the Gin bottle in his cabinet behind him.

"You know what?" He whispered to the bottle of Gin, "She has been jealous for years." And finally cut the desk light off. "Good night, see you next time."

*   *   *

Honolulu, Hawaii

Kalargo's car cruised smoothly on the highway at eighty miles per hour. He was tempted to go faster, but he was the only driver on the road at two forty five in the morning. He slowed down to fifty five; he received a call from an old friend that suggested that he meet him at the cafe off the highway. Even though he had not seen him in awhile, he felt like he had always been trustworthy, so why not?

The cafe practically empty and spooky under the circumstances he parked and entered. He sighed as he sat at the counter. The waitress asked, "Need a menu?" She reached for the menu.

He stopped her, "No, just a cup of coffee please." He looked around while he waited. He stretched.

"Sugar?"

"Ummm, yeah and milk."
The waitress gave him a spoon and a napkin and went to get cream. He used the napkin to clean up, but he noticed some writing on the other side. He flipped it over. He thought it was very strange, he found it to be strange because it was in Chinese. He quickly looked around. He read it, "Someone is dirty among you, clean house immediately!"

His eyes opened wide. He stood up and tossed two

dollars on the counter and stormed out the café, "Too spooky." He felt as he jumped in the car and sped off.

On the way home he thought about each and every guy that worked for him in the past and to this date. He smiled because Stacy kept popping up on his mind, but he knew he had to focus.

Moments later, he arrived to his house. He tiptoed through the living room. The TV on, he cut it off. The guest room door was open, he closed it. He quietly crawled in bed like a sneaky snake. Jamie was sound asleep, naked, beautiful, and desirable. She was awakening by his wet tongue on her ankle and up her calf. She smiled and played like she was so sleepy. He knew how to wake her up and he did it very well. They made love through bout the night.

The next morning sun slowly moved between the shades and across Stacy's face.

"Ahhh…" She moaned.

"My head," it pounded like a bass drum as she lay in bed on her back holding her head, "I must have had way too much to drink." She lifted the sheets. She never got out of her clothes.

"I can't handle anymore of these wild nights." She mumbled, looked around and realized that she was still at Kalargo's house. She was in the bathroom when she overheard Jamie and him making love. She leaned over the sink and sighed.

She was sad deep down inside. She couldn't have a relationship that lasted more than two or three weeks. The relationship would end the first night of copulation. She buried her face in her palms and sucked up her depression, let out an aggravating sigh of relief. She had learned to ignore her feelings and move on with life.

Kalargo sat behind Jamie in the Jacuzzi bubbled with strawberry suds. He slowly washed, massage, and combed through her hair with his fingers. The shampoo lathered as he used more of it to wash and massage her back. He kissed her on the back of her neck. She leaned back and rested on his chest. She turned around and kissed him on the lips.

"I wish I could lie here all day." She put one leg out of the Jacuzzi. Suddenly she submerged herself and stood up, "but I know I can't." Her glossy body stood before him. She tiptoed into the shower to wash her hair of shampoo.

Moments later he remembered the napkin. He raised himself from the water and nakedly walked into the bedroom. His wet foot prints trailed his every move. The soap suds slowly slid down his shiny wet body. He grabbed his pants from the dirty clothes hamper.

"Damn." He read it again, "Someone is dirty among your crew. Clean up the coffee spill, he has priors." He stood there thinking, naked as a j bird. His wet hands soaked the napkin. He looked up at the ceiling.

"Need a towel?" He looked around as the towel landed on his shoulder. He wrapped it around his neck. He walked over to the night stand grabbed a lighter and thought about burning the napkin.

He pulled his pants up his legs and grabbed a white t-shirt. With the receiver in his hand, he dialed Bennett's number.

"Yeah, hello."

"Hey Bennett, wake up!" He commanded.

"I am, awake."

"What happened last night?" He walked into the bathroom to brush his teeth.

"I did exactly what you told me. I bailed Damion out, and I am going to bail the others out right now." He paused, "What time is it?"

"Twelve thirty." He spoke with a mouth full of toothpaste and toothbrush in his hand.

"Hold on." He could hear him coughing and clearing his throat and chest. "Babe, get up and get breakfast going. It's going to be another long day." Bennett told his wife in the back ground, "Yeah I'm back, now Damion, seem to be cool.
He didn't say anything and they didn't ask him much either." He took a drag from his cigarette, "You know Kalargo, I think they knew he was a new guy, a truck driver that picked up and delivered. You know what I mean?"

"Hmmm, yeah." He gargled and spat out tooth paste and mouth wash. He thought about telling him about the napkin.

"How did they know about the warehouse?" There was silence.

"No idea, only reason I got away. I was standing by the escape tunnel." There was a pause and a question.

"So what's next Kalargo?"

He walked out the bathroom, "Hmmm, go bail out the other two; after wards make sure you bring them both to me. At the same time, I got some checking around to do.", before he ended the call, "oh yeah, Bennett! Make sure." He repeated himself, "make sure that you are not followed. They may put a tail on them." They both agreed.

"Bring them to Burger King on Nue Nue st." The call ended.

As he placed the phone down, He could hear the TV and stereo on from the living room. He knew Jamie was in the closet getting dressed.

"Jamie, go and ask Stacy if she's going to eat breakfast. If not..." He reached for his shoes. "Are you hungry?" He asked her.

She exited the closet with a pair of jean shorts, "We are going to get a bite to eat, how these look?"

He looked over his shoulder as he dug into the drawer for socks, "Absolutely stunning."

She walked over and kissed him.

"Well I guess I'll get something on the go." He said.

She grabbed her keys and purse, "I'll call you later."

She left with Stacy.

＊   ＊   ＊

The sun beamed through Kalargo's windshield as he kept a paranoid eye on the inmate release at the Honolulu jail. He parked a half a block away to make sure Bennett was not followed. The first thirty minutes was crucial. He blast the air condition hoping it would stop the trail of sweat that crawl down his back. He debated in his mind if he should take a chance of going to use the bathroom.

"Damn, I knew I should have used it before I left." He pushed down on his mid section and looked in his driver side mirror. He grabbed a piece of gum and tossed it in his mouth and mumbled as he chewed his gum.

He reclined his seat and adjusted his mirror. He sighed and nervously looked in all his mirrors and looked at his watch.

"Five more minutes." He looked around and spotted a cafe that he could duck into to use the bathroom. He tapped his left foot against the bottom of the driver door.

"What the hell. I can run in and be out." He mumbled and opened the door. The sound of traffic and the smell of the downtown came to life. The exhaust of a cement truck slapped him as he dipped across the street and into the cafe. He weaved his way through the line.

"Excuse me, bathroom?" he pointed his finger.

"It's out of order." The employee said.

He rolled his eyes and turned around for the door. He step outside and immediately looked towards the jail. He walked funny, desperate and noticed an alley across the street.

"Thank God!" He quickly held his hand up at the moving traffic to jay walk, "Hey sorry." He waved at the driver. In the middle of the street was when he saw a patrolman watching him.

"Great, ahh no." he saw Bennett, Steve, and Pat

shaking hands with the bondsman. He quickly turned around and rushed back to his car. He sighed.

"Damn it! About time they come out!" He jumped in and cranks the car, blew a bubble as he looked in the driver mirror.

"Come on!" he inclined his seat.

He put his car in drive and just before he could drive off. The patrolman tapped on his window. He looked at him and signaled to roll down the window. He nearly pissed on himself.

"Shit. Shit. Shit." He slowly rested his head on the head rest.

"How can I help you Mr. Police officer?" He looked like he had piss up to his eyes.

The officer stepped back from the car.

He looked Samoan, big and well tanned with curly short hair. He was very big, perhaps closer to fat and fighting to stay in his little brother's uniform. He looked very cultural. He smiled. He held his frown tightly.He held his pad in his hand and pulled his pen from his shirt.

Kalargo was tapping his foot nonstop.

"This is a fine automobile. Is this one of those new Lexus's LS400?"

He was in shock and a little pissed, "Yeah."

"Bro I like this car. I was thinking of getting my daughter one of these. You know for her graduation. How does it ride, pretty fast?"

Kalargo looked in his mirror, "Hmmm, Super fast" He anxiously said.

"I saw you earlier. You looked kind of lost."

"Well, I am a little lost. Do I make a left or right to get to the hospital?" He looked at Bennett's car drive by. He quickly answered his own question, "Now I remember a left and two blocks on the right." He looked up at the officer.

"You got it right." He noticed a car parking in front of a fire hydrant, "You have a nice day." He went from a fan to an officer of the law.

He followed Bennett trying to notice a tailing undercover car, nothing. "So far so good." he mumbled.

It took thirty minutes to get to the Burger King. He dialed Bennett's number.

"Bennett, what's going on?" He parked several blocks away after carefully driving around, "It's cool baby, just here waiting for you to call. I didn't think you would show." He sighed and sipped on a vanilla milk shake.

"Well what's going on?" He closed his car door and walked towards the Burger King.

"They have a court date."

"Who's the judge?" He waited for a response. He could hear him asking them in the back ground.

"Judge Kalauani, does he ring a bell?"

"Well, let's just say thank God it's him." He laughed and sat down across the street from the Burger King and looked for anything out of the normal.

"Let's say him and my father are golfing buddies. We can take care of him."
He pulled a seat and thought about how crooked he is.

"I'll handle it from here. Everybody go home and wait for my call. I'll have the lawyers drop some names and get this thrown out."

*   *   *

Under clear blue western skies that were being chased by darkness from the east. The sun descended slowly. The purple and yellowish red eye danced on the horizon. The brightest stars can be seen as the flight from South Korea circle the island of Oahu.

"Ding ding." The fasten seat belt light illuminated. The captain's voice was calm over the intercom.

"Ladies and Gentlemen, I would like to welcome you to Honolulu, Hawaii. The weather is currently 89 degrees with a slight breeze out of the north. I hope you have enjoyed your flight to the southern pacific islands of paradise. We should be landing in twenty five minutes." The captain pointed out the different islands of Hawaii and a little bit of history about them.

Mugumbi stretched and lifted his blind to his window. He reached for the air plane's phone. He slid his credit card through the slot and started dialing. His Korean was warm to hear and his wife was excited to talk to him.

"Hello. " She was still in bed.

"Just letting you know that the plane will be touching down soon."
She loved his accent in Korean, but she never knew it was a voice of a hit man.

"I love you." She said.

"I love you. I'll be back in a week, may be sooner." He put his seat belt on.

"I'll be waiting." She gave him a kiss over the phone and they ended the call.

Chapter 8

The sweat dripped from Kalargo's body as he strained to push 270 lbs off his chest. His veins were like roots from a three hundred year old tree. He trembled as he slowly pushed the bar. He didn't have a spotter to help him. He found the inner strength and concentration to clear the stand. His heavy breathing pushed small amounts of sweat from around his lips, as he sat up and hung his head between his chests, resting his elbows on his upper thigh. He deeply planted his thumbs on his temples and massaged his headache, looked around his weight room and sighed. He used his fore arm to wipe his face. He was stunned.

"What the hell…" His forearm was smeared with blood. He ran over to the mirror. "Damn." He grabbed a towel. Lately his nose bleeds and headaches started to reoccur. He relaxed and held his head back with the towel on his nose. Before leaving he noticed CNN news was talking about the Persian Gulf and Iraq invasion of Kuwait.

"It's shameful how they focus on all of this oil. When there are many countries at war. But because they have nothing to truly contribute to the world…" He shook his head in a disappointed way. "…they are over looked, thousands die without help, but then again this is sadly my way of making money." He walked into the living room.

He checked the towel for blood. "Someone has to help the poorest people in the world." He claimed.

"They are sending five hundred thousand troops. For what, oil?" He sucked air between his beautiful white teeth. "I've sent ammo to over thirty countries that have been at war for more than five years, but no one jumped in to stop the mass killings in none of those countries." He checked his nose and grabbed a bottle of water.

"Yep, let them keep worrying about the powerful countries. I'll keep making my money." He said as he nodded his head at a shameful game the world plays. As he passed through the living room he pushed play to hear Anita Baker while he took a long hot bath. He lit the candles, ran the water and plucked nose hairs. He applied his shaving cream.

*   *   *

"Room four fifty five please." Mugumbi checked into his hotel. The receptionist gave him a key without question.

"Enjoy your vacation." She smiled. She didn't know it, but she had just ruined his moment. He hated people that displayed a fake smile.

He nodded his head, "Thank you."

He found his room, slid his key, and opened the door. He looked in the bathroom, closets, and under the bed. Finally he looked under the mattress and pulled a small black case that contained a .380 caliber revolver and silencer. He looked at his watch and walked over to the T.V. and turned it on. He scans the channels for his favorite South Korean program.

The United States seemed so different to him. He had grown accustom to the South Korean way of life. However, Hawaii catered to the Japanese tourist.

"Found it." He always amazed Americans when he spoke Korean better than he spoke English. He entered the bathroom and looked in the mirror. He rubbed his fingers across his mustache, pushed his lip up to inspect his gums. He licked his lips to moisturize them. He looked down at his arm and touched his needle tracks. One by one he touched them like his temple had been destroyed. For the first time he realized how ugly and embarrassing they were. He wore long sleeve shirts to hide them.

He spent some time in the bathroom. The hotel phone rang; he walked over to answer it. His beloved dope in his right hand and picked up the receiver. He sat down on the bed and listened. Finally he hung the receiver on the phone. He walked over to open the door. There was no one; he saw an exit door down the hall. He quickly grabbed his .380, loaded it and slid it in his front right pocket. He ran towards the exit and hid.

Behind the exit door, he peeped through the crack of the door. "Hmm…" he raised his eye brows out of curiosity. He saw a twenty five year old, short curly black hair,

Polynesian decent.

He stopped in front of Mugumbi's hotel room door, without hesitation he pulled an eight by twelve mustard envelope from beneath his shirt and slid it beneath the door. He quickly ran down the hall and disappeared. For the first time he actually saw who the messenger was. He made sure it was clear before coming from behind the exit door. In his room he retrieved the envelope that contained a map, itinerary, photo, and directions to the location of his victim.

He pulled the picture out and sat down at the desk. The light from the window entered that side of the room. He leaned forward, resting his elbows and studied the picture. He wanted to remember as much as possible, like the scar beneath the bridge of his nose.

After an hour of preparation, he grabbed the receiver, and dialed 0, "Yes, this the front desk of the Marriott Waikiki how can I help you?"

"Yes I would like to have a rental car to go sightseeing."

"Are you interested in a small, compact or economy?"

He thought about it. "Do you have a four door sedan?"

"I can check, give me one moment please. Can you hold?"

"Yes." He held the photo in his hand.

"Yes we do, we have the Chrysler cirrus." There was a silence. He had no idea what the Chrysler cirrus was, but it sounded good.

"Yeah I'll be down to pick it up in thirty minutes."
They both agreed and ended the call. He quickly primped,
and left the room.

He wanted to be as familiar with the area as much as
possible and with the victim's daily movement. The target
lived in a high rise condo on Ala Wai blvd, a busy one
way that becomes quiet after one thirty in the morning.
The canal that separated Waikiki from Honolulu had a golf
course that stretched the length of the canal. He is
nocturnal creature of the night. His favorite place on the
weekend is a popular club by the name of Candy Paint. He
was known to be heavily drunk, and flamboyant.

He drove down the Blvd checking every alley, garbage
dumpster, nook and cranny. He looked for cameras, smoke
areas and parking garages. He looked at his watch. The
hour hand was on the nine and the minute hand was
slightly on the six. He pulled over to the right and grabbed
his bag of bread to feed the ducks. He wanted to walk and
learn the area. He may have to jump in the canal and run
across the golf course to get away. He wore a pair of lose
fitted cotton shorts, golfer's wide brim hat, with sandals
that buckled around his ankle. His gun was tucked
between his belt in the back of his pants. He walked for
two hours before he decided to walk to the club.

*   *   *

The next morning the sun rose between the mountains
and played peak-a- boo with the clouds. Some parts of
Honolulu were damped from passing showers. Mugumbi
lay in bed tossing and turning from a dream. He spoke in
his native tongue. He woke up reaching for his right thigh
and realized there were knocking at the door. He sighed.

His eyes opened as he heard the lock on the door
opening.

"Room service."

"Good morning…" He quickly slid the gun in the pocket of his Marriott robe.

"Room service?" She asked.

"Hmm…" He stood and slowly asked for her to come in.

"It's not a problem, I could come back later if you prefer?" her timid manner and voice was cute. He walked over to the window and sat down holding his leg. He rubbed the scars that had not healed properly.

"You need ice on that?" The maid said as she entered the bathroom.

"No, it's not as bad as it looks." He walked over to remove his travel bag from the edge of the bed.

"Lesson learned." he said to the maid.

She peaked from the bathroom. "Excuse me."

He felt like talking since she had seen him touching his leg.

"The scar, I said that it was a lesson learned." He opened the travel bag.

"And what was that?" She said and returned to cleaning the bathroom.

"The lesson learned was to always be careful with your enemies." He laughed and she didn't get it. He stuffed the eight by twelve envelope under his arm and walked out the room.

When he returned, the room was cold, cleaned and scented. He tossed his news paper on the bed, unbuckled his belt and pulled it from around his waist. He opened his needle kit and sat on the edge of the bed next to the night stand. He put a small amount of water on his crooked shaped spoon. Like a scientist, he carefully added his heroin to the water and heated the spoon with a lighter. The flamed darken it black as the substance bubbled. From the spoon to the syringe he put it, quickly grabbed the belt and tightens it around his upper bicep. He put the end of the belt in between his teeth to hold it. He pulled harder until his veins looked like a batch of muddy earth worms.

He sighed as the rush of dope made its way through his body. He sat there thinking about the feeling, the warmth and love that followed.

*   *   *

Seoul, South Korea

In the eyes of a fifteen inch gold fish that swam toward the glass of a beautiful fish tank. It looked forward to being fed. Na Min stood with food in his hand, "Here Topi, I don't know if I'm feeding you too much or too little." He tossed food in the tank; Topi swam to the top to gobble the crumbs.

He turned his back to the huge exotic fish tank that held some of the world's rarest fish. "Damn what's taking him so long to call me?" He looked at his watch. "He's late."

He walked over to his desk to make a decision. He decided to wait for Zang's phone call. "Honey if the phone ring, take a message, I'll be …" He was interrupted by the phone, without hesitation. "Hello."

117

"Yeah, Na Min, I hope I did not have you waiting?"Zang sighed. "We have a small problem," he paused.

"What kind of a problem?" Na Min's asked.

There were silence and then a huge sigh that warmed his earpiece. "Well as you know we have invested a lot of money in this country. Our people are not, how can I say it? They don't quite fit in. They stand out like pink tigers."

Na Min sat down and tapped his eraser of his pencil on the desk top calendar. He broke the silence. "Other words, you would like to have, perhaps a black…" He swallowed his fear of his request. "…person." The tapping stopped and the pencil fell from his hand. He rubbed his thumb across his eyebrows and slowly pushed his hand to the back of his neck and massaged it.

"Zang, I don't have anyone who is qualified with the military experience." He leaned back into the seat. "That is a lot to be asking for Zang. Do you know people are watching me? They are suspicious. Do you think I have people that I can just pluck from my hand for this kind of stuff?" He closed his eyes.

"Listen, we trust you and it's the only reason we are asking you. We trust your decisions and we are willing to make it worth your while." Zang said.

"Zang, you think you guys have all the answers. This year is supposed to be our final operation. But now you call me with all this. I don't know what to make of it. I mean, come on. What do you think this is Zang?" He threw the pencil across the desk with anger, "I just can't believe this." He poured a glass of Gennifer and slammed it down his throat.

"Na Min, I swear we are planning to make this our final request of you. You have delivered throughout the years and you have had some close calls and hairy situations. We are willing to compensate you for everything you have done for us."

His breathing can slightly be heard; before he could speak he was interrupted.

"How would you like to mysteriously inherit a two million dollar apt building?" He waited for him to respond.

"How important is this so call, black person? What do you need him to do?"

"Well, we need someone who could go in undetected, speak the native language good enough to pass as one of their own, and we are willing to train him if we need to." He paused.

"And the mission of this person?" he knew he preferred not to talk about it.

"We need to give an executive party to the General Kakambo Twigani."

He realized how heavy this was and the difference it would make to the war. The North Koreans were no longer trying to just make money from the diamonds and oil. They were trying to perhaps colonize and control this small African country.

The sound of the Gin came from the bottle as he poured another glass. "Zang, Zang, my God what are you trying to…" He held the receiver from his ear and choked it with his hands and gritted his teeth. He calmly put the receiver back to his ear. He sighed. He leaned forward and planted his elbows on the desk.

"How long before the drilling will begin for oil and diamonds?" He asked him.

"Well, that is a part of the problem. A lot of things can't get done unless the war is over, but, if we don't have control over the situation. One of the NATO countries will eventually step in and gain control and discover the natural resources."

"How many apt buildings do you have?"

Zang grunted, "Plenty in the United States and in other countries."

"I tell you what. I want three apt buildings at ten million inherited to me." He said.

"So, this means you can deliver?" His desperate voice of urgency was slowly relieved.

"Listen, we will go over everything in greater detail." Na Min said.

"Hmm... We need someone soon, like in the next three weeks." He said with concern.

"Zang, relax and wait for my phone call." He ended the call.

*   *   *

It was nine thirty and Mugumbi's mind was made up to where the hit will take place. He figured he would follow him and park down the street from the club.

He looked in his rear view mirror, finally he saw the black Benz pull out from the condominium.

"OK." He waited until he passed him, looked to verify license plate number. "That is it."

After two hours, he was frustrated. The prospector stopped four different places before arriving to the club, he knew if allowed his frustration to get involved something could go wrong. It was one thirty in the morning when they arrived at the club, now came the wait.

Chapter 9

The parking garage of the club was located among a plaza of stores, three stories high and very spacious.

"Ding, ding." The elevator door opened and the club customers giggled as they looked for their cars.

"I hope this is the right floor." She was obviously drunk and leaned on the shoulder of her girlfriend. Their voices echoed as the clacking of their hills tapped and scratched the concrete. The voices silenced as they walked further away from him. The sound of keys dangled and the laughter can barely be heard.

He looked at his watch, and sighed. "It's almost about that time." He wiped a bead of sweat from his nose. His black golf gloves were skin tight. He also thought the garage could be a bad place to make this happened. The crowd continued to exit the elevator and walk to their cars. He ducked, a couple walked from the floor below searching for their car. The keys are heard opening the car door. Their lips locked with a French kiss. One thing lead to another, it did not take long for the windows to fog. She moaned softly but the movement of the car was inevitable.

"Ding ding." A group of people walked off the elevator. "Look!" They were in shock. "God, Oh my." They giggled as they stared at the couple and rushed toward their cars.

More people passed them and finally they cranked their car up and left. Not many cars remained on this floor, and again the prospector took forever. Suddenly the elevator door opened and the man on the photo exited. He whistled, as he retrieved his keys from his pocket.

"Good nobody is around." faced down in front of the victims car. He pulled out his gun and twisted the silencer on tightly. The echoes of his whistling stopped. Mugumbi's heart pounded his chest so hard it felt like it was in slow motion. He did not know if he had been seen or not, but it was an uncomfortable feeling. The victim stopped to where only his shoes could be seen. He appeared to be looking around. Finally, he slowly walked cautiously as if he was suspicious.

Just before he pulled the trigger, suddenly a car horn blasted the parking garage.

"Oh my God!" it startled him. A loud voice came from a far.

"Long time no see."

"Wow, Mr. Kobalulu. How long has it been? At the least, what? Five years." They hugged and spoke for awhile. Their conversation was unintelligible. They laughed as they said their goodbyes.

"Come on." He waited for his friend to drive off, wet his lips, gripped the handled on his gun.

He inhaled deeply, closed his eyes and listened to his footsteps. The sound of the car keys dangled. It was so quiet, peaceful, and sudden. The sound of the silencer was so vacuumed like and just powerful. The victim fell over in his car.

"Perfect." He walked by and quickly closed the door with his hip. He looked around the garage and shook his head. He looked into the car and shot him two more times in the head to make sure he was dead, and walked away unnoticed.

*   *   *

Kalargo covered his head with his pillow. The phone rang; he tried to ignore it by pushing a button on the night stand to shut off the ringers on all the phones in the house. Ten minutes later, his cellular phone was ringing. He also turns it off as he mumbled and cussed, "It's probably Jamie."

Fifteen minutes later, his pager goes off, "God damn it!" he snatched his pager and looked at it. "No way…" he turns the phones on and dialed Mugumbi's number. They spoke in their native tongue, "…hey uncle. It has been awhile. You picked a good time to call."

"Well I was in town for a couple of days, so I decided to visit my nephew."

He pulled the pillow over his face and looked at the clock. "Hmmm, it's ten in the morning." He swallowed a dry throat. "I needed to get up anyway." He gave him directions to where he lived.

Later that day

As Mugumbi walked out of Kalargo's house, Bennett walked up the driveway.

"Uncle this is my number one guy, Bennett. This is my Uncle I always tell you about." They shook hands.

"South Korea, right yeah he speaks of you. It's a pleasure to meet you. Hey I'll be inside." Bennett made his way in the house.

"Yeah go ahead."

After ten minutes Kalargo came in. "I got some information."

"What you got?" Bennett ask.

He pulled out a photo of Saul. "Do you recognize him?"

"Yeah, he used to work for me. Where did you…" before he could say another word, he showed him a note, "I found this on my windshield." He gave him the note.

"Wow." He gave him the note back and told him to wait a moment. He told him about the napkin from the café.

"What does it mean, you have a spill?" Bennett ask.

"Clean up the dirty spill, someone is dirty among you." They both looked at each other and shook their heads. Bennett rubbed his bottom lip with his left thumb and sighed.

"And he left out of the blue, no reason at all; you know what we have to do?" Kalargo looked at him. "This is the rat that had the warehouse raided." He grunted.

"How do you know?" Bennett wanted to be for sure.

Kalargo sat down to explain, "Check this out the same night the warehouse was raided. I received a phone call from an old friend of mine. He told me to meet him at the cafe. It was important. But when I got there, I waited, ordered coffee. Somehow, this note manages to come with my coffee. The waitress had no idea how it got there."

"So who is the old friend?" Bennett ask.

Kalargo's right index finger pointed toward the ceiling, "I can't say. If he went through this much trouble to let me know this. It would be best to keep him anonymous." They both agreed.

That was one of the good qualities that he liked about Bennett, If he did not try to know more than what he needed to know.

"So this is the guy?"

"Got to be." Kalargo assured him.

"Are we sure?" Bennett looked at him.

"All of this can't be a coincidence."

"I guess he got it coming." Bennett sat down and sighed. "Just say when boss."

"Go ahead and go home, I'll call you later to night when I get the address on this guy." Bennett stood and walked himself out.

Later that night

Bennett opened the door of the Kalargo's old mustard green 1970 impala. The interior was dated, the rust on the outside made its way to the inside. The motor sounded like a sewing machine, but the overall appearance was downright ugly.

"Wow, you are really trying to be low key, aren't you?" he laughed. "Where in the hell did you get this from?"

He smiled, "A guy at a junk yard. They were giving it away." before he could respond, "Hey, you have everything? I don't want to have to return for anything."

"Yep." He looked at his disguise, fake tattoo on his neck, curly hair wig and paste on beard. They both looked like they were flash back disco seventy kids.

"So where does he live?" Bennett ask.

"The other side of the island there is a small house in the middle of nowhere." He made a left turn as the sound of the blinker ended. "He lives by himself."

"So how you want to do this?" Bennett scratched the back of neck.

"I don't know but it depends on my feelings." He cracked the window to allow the highway wind to cool his scalp. He looked at the dash board clock, and down between his legs were his black gloves. He grabbed one and used his right knee to steer the car at seventy miles an hour. He pulled the glove over his right hand and then the left.

"Go ahead and put your gloves on, I got this." He pointed at a bottle of general purpose cleaning spray," Go ahead and wipe down everything, that way if we have to run, our finger prints won't be in the car."

That was one of the qualities he like about Kalargo, he was smart, and on top of his shit.

"If you have to sneeze, don't. But if you have to, do it on your sleeve, better yet, in your shirt." As he was talking Bennett pulled out a pack of cigarette, "And if you have to smoke…" he paused and looked at him. "…swallow the butt of the cigarette."

"Yeah right…" He pulled out a cigarette and put it between his lips. He looked at him.

"That cigarette will get you one or the other, prison time, or killed."

Bennett slowly and unwillingly pulled the cigarette from his lips like a lollypop had been snatch from a kid. He looked out the window and looked at all the palms trees that started to look like long haired cigarettes. He placed the cigarette above his ear. He sighed.

"Are you serious?" He asked him as the cigarette palm trees passed his window.

"DNA, it has sent more people to prison than any witness. Hey we'll be there in five minutes."

The entry from the highway down this dark road was perfect. They parked the car and retrieved a bat, two pistols, and rope.

The lights up stairs had just turned off. The television was the only thing that was visible. They both stood outside and planned how they would gain entry into the house.

"Are you sure that there isn't anyone home?" Bennett asked him as he slid the pistol into his right back pocket.

He sighed, "Well…" He scratched his head. "…if it is." He rubbed his nose with his left hand, "We can't leave any witnesses."

"But, it shouldn't be." He led the way towards the front door. Their voices were at a whisper.

"On three, we kick the door in and run up stairs." They both nodded.

"One, two…" Before they counted to three, a person came down the stairs. It was him. They looked at each other. They started the count over.

The huge noise of the door crashing down, glass shattered everywhere scared Saul. He dropped his glass and before he could reach for a weapon. A pistol was on top of his upper lip.

"Don't move." Bennett said with a crooked smile. His mask covered his face, but his eyes stared him down.

"You snitch ass mother fucker."

Saul tried to explain. "What!" His fat jiggled like an ornament on a windy day. His white shorts sagged, the sleeveless shirt revealed his hairy armpits, his chest hairs protruded out the v cut shirt. His huge feet looked stressed from the three hundred and ninety pound body weight that gave him hard time breathing.

"Sit your ass down!" Kalargo said.

The table was behind him. A fresh cup of hazel nut coffee and plate of ginger cookies sat untouched. He had returned to get his night snack.

"Man, what is this. What you want, money? Look I got money!" He pushed his shoulders upward like money was no problem.

Kalargo held his head back and let out a huge sigh of relief. From the bottom of his throat he pulled off the mask.

Saul fell from the chair as he tried to crawl away from him. "Kalargo! What are you doing here?"

He walked around the table. Saul eyes followed his every move. He tried to read his mind.

"Are these fresh?" He picked up the plate of cookies.

"Yeah, go ahead have some." He was so scared.

"I still can't think of a reason." Bennett stood between them both until Kalargo walked completely around and leaned on the out dated kitchen counter. He looked around and noticed how he was living. He took a bite into one of the cookies, and tossed the rest in his mouth.

"Oh my God, Did you bake these?" He tried to catch a fallen crumb.

"Bennett, you can take off the mask now. I know it's uncomfortable."

"Yeah" he pulled it off, "it's hot as hell in here." His sweat ran down his neck, fanning himself to cool off.

"Listen, this is not what you think it is. I can explain." He was interrupted.

"How long have you had this house?"

He looked puzzled. "Little over three years."

"Hey, Bennett you want a cookie?" He turned it down, "They don't make cookies like these in my home country, are you sure you baked these? You mean to tell me that there is no other person here?" Kalargo wiped his mouth with his forearm.

"I swear I baked them." Saul breathing was in between his words.

Kalargo turned his back, "Now it's a shame that I had to come out here on this occasion." However, he turned around with his mouth filled with cookies, "Damn, I think I am addicted to these cookies." He held one cookie in his hand. He walked over to Saul.

"I know you didn't think I was going to hog all of the cookies did you?" He walked over to him.

"I got two choices for you. Deed me the property and we could act as if this never happened."

Before he could finish, "Yeah anything Kalargo, whatever you want!" He begged him. His fat face gave him a sad clown look.

"Or you could give me the recipe for these cookies and maybe." He paused a minute. "Just maybe, we could work something out." Before he could finish, Saul fell to the floor like a struggling whale begging to go back out to sea. From his knees he started yelling out the recipe.

"Shhhh, hey it's no way I could remember that, come on man." Kalargo was smiling.

"Hey sit back in the chair." It took him two minutes to climb his ass back into the chair that creaked and moaned that it may break into pieces any moment. He looked back at the counter at the plate. One cookie left. He reached for it, just before he bit it. He asked him if he wanted it. He hesitated, but he said yeah nervously. In the palm of the black glove was the last cookie.

"Milk?" he asked him. He nodded his head.

"Now I really did not come here to hear all these excuses. You understand me?" he cleared his nostril, "Now you have two choices right?"

"But out of those two, which one you think I want?" He looked him dead in his eyes. The shape of the cookie can damn near be seen going down his throat.

"The house?" he looked at him.

He stood back and open his eyes and hands as if he guessed the right answer. He pulled out some documents and told him to sign them.

"So for what you have done. And you know…" He threw up his hands like it was obvious. I am going to punish you forever to be poor." He scratched his head.

Bennett looked at him like he was crazy.

Saul looked relieved. "So if I sign them, everything would be
forgotten about?"

"Did you, drink some milk?" He pointed at the milk.

Saul quickly grabbed the cup and drank it empty; milk spilled from his bottom lip and ran into the valley and creeks of his fat flaky rolls of caked up dirt around his neck.

"Oh yeah, how much money you have?" Kalargo paced the kitchen floor. He pulled down on the bottom of his gloves to tighten them.

"I have six hundred thousand under the stair case." He pointed to the key on the wall. "That's the key, the brown one."

He gave him the ink pen. "You did well, especially with the cookies."

"Bennett, keep an eye on him. I'll go check the stair case out."

It took him five minute to pull out the huge duffel bags of money out from the staircase. He walked back into the kitchen sweating like he had run a marathon.

"Jesus Christ, you were not lying." He looked at his watch. He knew he only had about five more minutes before the cyanide pill would kick in.

"Bennett, give me a hand with these bags."

"What about…" He started to ask.

He peeked into the kitchen, looked at Bennett and then at Saul. He waved his hand and looked at his watch.

"He'll be fine." He returned to the stare case.

They carried the two duffel bags to the car. They were breathing hard, sweating through their clothes. "Come on lets go." He told him.

The ride back was peaceful; Bennett reached over and turned the radio on. He sighed and pulled out a cigarette. He kept his mouth shut and waited for him to say something.

Kalargo looked in the mirror for any followers. "Bennett, when we get to where we are going, take one of the bags for yourself. But whatever you do. Don't let anyone know you got it." He looked at him. He agreed to it.

"Do me another favor, let the window down?" Bennett responded, "Not a problem."

Chapter 10

"Listen!" Na Min vehemently said. "Your Honor, this warehouse is owned by the U.S. Navy, which is two miles down the road. Everything inside of it belongs to training exercise that is top secret. The FBI had been given a bad lead. Yes! I do appreciate their duties and professionalism. However a bad lead does not give them the right to confiscate, interfere with a government training exercise." He looked the federal judge directly into his eyes. "I really need you to look the other way, drop the case."

As they sat over a dinner that had not been touched, He slid an envelope that held an undisclosed amount of cash.

"Done?" He held his hand on top of it.

The judge sighed; He quickly pulled the envelope from the table. He shook his head, "Consider it done."

He had learned a long time ago to always cover his own ass. As he walked out the restaurant, he pulled from his coat pocket a digital voice recorder and turned it off.

As he walked towards the street, he reached for his phone and dialed Kalargo's cell.

"Yes hello."

"Hold on, let me get off the other line." He clicked over to Jamie.

"Hey Jamie it's my father. I will call you after I talk to him." She pouted and he clicked over.

"Kalargo."

"Yes I am here." He sighed and wondered what he wanted to talk to him about. He hoped that it had nothing to do with Saul's murder.

"Listen, I wanted to talk to you about a project that requires your caliber of expertise." Na Min paused.

Kalargo stood up and walked into his master suite. "Hmm, hold on. Is it anything like Jakarta?"

"Oh no, no, no nothing like Jakarta." He grinned.

"But it does, hey listen. I'm in Hawaii. Most of what I need to tell you. I prefer to speak to you in person. What are you doing in one hour?"

He looked at his watch, "That will be, ten thirty." He sighed. "Where would you like to meet? You know you are always welcome to come over to my place." Kalargo suggested.

"You live to far, and it is late. I have a flight in the morning." He sighed. "Meet me at the bar that we always meet at. Say no later than ten forty five." They agreed and the line ended.

He quickly called Jamie. "Hey…"

She was excited. "Wow that was fast."

"We have a change in plans. My father is in Hawaii and he says he needs to speak to me in person. Hmmm, maybe I can meet you after I finish talking to him."

"Or maybe you could pick me up on your way to meet him. I'm sure he would be happy to see us together." She could hear it in his voice that it might not be a good idea.

"No, how about we meet at eleven thirty at the bar. You know the same bar we met at before."

She remembered, "OK eleven thirty. I'll be there." They ended the line.

*   *   *

The club Le Femme was partly crowded, it was eleven o'clock, and from a distance it looked like the conversation that they were having was secretive, and they appeared to not agree on what they talked about.

The dancers were nude as they fondled one another. The fog smoke from the stage spilled over. The lights flashed with different colors, and the music blared loud enough to drown people's conversations into secrecy. In a corner booth a waitress walked over with their third round of drinks. She placed them down and expected her tip. She was topless, heavy set rack that looked fake, but perfect. Kalargo gave her a two dollar tip so she could leave.

"No! You mean to tell me that," He raised his shoulders and opened his eyes to amazement. "You... out of all people can't find someone to go over and do this?" He pushed his diet coke away from him. He sighed and took notice to the dancers.

"Listen, it's not that I or we can't find someone else. The matter is." He took a drink from his gin and orange juice. "We want or prefer someone whom we can trust."

He sat back with his drink in his hand, "Mugumbi, what about him?"

"Too old, we need someone young, which can easily fit into the population. I mean, you are exactly what we need."

He sipped from the glass of diet coke, "You know... this is worse than Jakarta. This is insane." He leaned back and rested his head, let out a huge sigh. He rubbed his face with his left hand vigorously.

"How long is this supposed to take?" Kalargo looked at him.

"No more than two weeks, you'll be in and out." Na Min told him.

He smiled and laughed at an inside joke, "That sound like what I told Jamie when I first met her." They both grinned.

He threw up his hands, "What am I suppose to tell Jamie? Oh my God, you know this is not something I was expecting to hear. Jamie is going to flip. How am I suppose to get in The Gambia?" before he could say another word. "This sounds like a bad idea to me."

Na Min slammed the rest of his drink down his throat and flagged for the waitress. "Well..." He raised his palms to try to calm him down. "First of all, you will have to fly down to the Philippines for training. That will be at least a week, or two." He hoped he was not counting the weeks as he spoke.

"Then we have special transportation that will deliver you to where ever you need to go. From there you will have to parachute into the Gambia under the night sky." Na Min paused.

Kalargo's eyes opened wide, "Parachute?"

"Hold on, you will have everything you would need." He was interrupted.

"Will there be like helpers that I can meet with while I am there?"

He looked him in his eyes, "Unfortunately, once you are there. You will be completely on your own." The waitress delivered more drinks.

"This…" he waited for her to leave. "…thank you, this sounds like a suicide mission. A no return deal." He sucked air through his pearly white teeth.

"Listen, if I thought that this was something you could not do, or the slightest chance that you would not return. I would not have brought this to you. You are my son, like a son. I gave you my last name. I raised you as if you were my own. This is coming from my heart. I am not saying that this will be a walk in the park. It won't be. This might be one of the most difficult things you will ever do." He was interrupted.

"How much am I going to be paid?" he sipped on his diet coke.

"Two million."

"Two million!" He looked at him with a surprising facial expression. He sighed and downed his drink. "Make it four million, and I'll go."

Na Min put his Genifer back down on the table. "You have a deal, but before I forget…" He held his right hand up to stop him. "…whatever you do, under no circumstance should you ever speak your native language. Never, never, and again never speak your native tongue."

"Is there a reason why?"

"You have two languages that you were born speaking. One of them is the one that you and Mugumbi speak. And then it is the other one that you hardly ever speak and only because you have no one to speak it with. However if someone speaks to you in this native tongue, you must. I cannot stress this enough. You must act like you have no idea what they are talking about. Do you hear me?" he grabbed his hand and looked him in the eyes.

"OK, I hear you. I have not spoken that tongue since I was a kid." He sighed.

He drum rolled his palms on the table, "So the General it is."

Suddenly Jamie walked over to the table, "Hello Na Min." She gave him a kiss on the cheek.

"He was surprised to see her. "Wow, isn't she beautiful." He looked at him. "No wonder you were crying earlier." He smiled at them both and looked at his watch.

"Wow, he looks at the time…" He stood from the table and slammed his drink.
"…well, it was a pleasure to see you again, Jamie." She stood and gave him a
hug. He cleared his throat, "Kalargo…" They hugged like father and son, "…you will be hearing from me very soon." He nodded his head as he walked towards the exit.

*   *   *

The next morning

Jamie walked out of the room half asleep. "Good

morning." She wore a night gown that barely came to her pubic hair. Her nipples were hard and she sighed because she was horny.

"Good morning." Kalargo replied without taking his eyes off the morning paper. The front page read, "Parking Garage Murder"

She grabbed a plastic cup and poured a glass of orange juice. "You want some?"

"Hmm, what are you having, orange juice?"

"Yes." She said.

"Why not, are you cooking breakfast?" She poured him a glass of orange juice and took it to him. "Well I could but I wanted to get some more sleep." She put the glass on the glass coffee table and headed back to the room. He tilted the paper and watched her ass cheeks bounce as she walked on her toes across the floor.

"I can wait till you wake up." He continued to read, looking for an article about Saul Kaapuluu's murder.

"Hmmm, nothing." he put the paper down, and drunk his orange juice. He stood up and paused. He noticed how horrible he felt. This nauseous feeling, headaches, and loose bowels that was uncontrollable. He let out a huge sigh and walked into his office. He fed the fish and talked to them.

"Hey big fella." he flopped into his corporate office chair and thought about Jamie, the trip to Africa, the circumstances, and the what if. He wondered how to tell Jamie. He thought it would be easier to some way include her, like having her manage the gym while he was gone. It sounded good. Perhaps watch over the house, check the mail, and make sure the lawn was cut, stuff like that.

"Yeah, ok." He turned around in the chair. "And don't forget, feed the fish."

He sat there thinking for three hours. He tapped his feet the entire time. But he was convinced, this is something he could do, and get away with it. He cracked his knuckles and the bones in his neck. He leaned forward and twisted his back to crack his bones along his vertebrae. He placed his elbows on his knees and placed his face in his palms.

"Damn it." He grabbed his bottom lip with his upper teeth and slowly let it slide away.

He stood up and walked out of his office. Moments later he slowly crawled into bed. Her warm body was soft, and desirable. He kissed her shoulder and she turned around and pulled him closer. They made passionate love and fell asleep in each other arms.

*   *   *

"Stop!" she screamed. She was having another bad dream. "Please." she cried.

He shook her until she was awake. "Jamie, wake up. You are having a bad dream."

She looked around with the sheets close to her face. She grabbed him and held him tightly.

"It's OK. You are safe."

"I keep having this dream of this black man hanging from this tree." She buried her face into the pillow. She wiped her tears, sighed and was happy it was just a dream.

"It just, seems so real." She shook her head. "So real,

like before, last time I had the same exact dream. This guy was hanging upside down from this huge tree." She swallowed her saliva to continue.

She sat up to face him. She looked him in his eyes. "Two men were beating him." Her facial expression was like she was really there. Her eyes widen as she told the dream. She turned around and sat with her legs crossed in the Indian position, "Why do I have these silly dreams?"

It was very obvious that she was frustrated. "Pass me…" She pointed at the orange juice.

"May be you seen a movie, perhaps awhile ago and somehow you are having these nightmares."

"No…" She shook her head, "…and then it's like I always have this dog that, somehow leads me to where this is happening." She explained.

He smiled, "You know what, not trying to be funny, but maybe you should just kill the dog." He nodded his head and they both laughed it off.

He comforted her, kissed her and made her laugh. He locked his lips with hers. She grabbed his mighty python and directed it into the passage of warmth that would lead to another round of passionate love.

Later that night, the phone rang and he answered it, " Hello."

"Sound like you're sleeping."

"Well…" before he could finish, "…I'm calling to tell that by morning you'll know when you will fly out to the Philippines. But go ahead and get your sleep, I'll let you know if the date is official."

He cleared his throat and said, "Ok." The line ended.

He looked over his shoulder and knew he would have to tell Jamie. But he let her sleep for now.

*   *   *

The next morning

Kalargo's office at the gym was filled with laughter. He told a funny story about Bennett. They held their sides, wiped their eyes of tears. He slammed his fist on his desk, "Stop! Stop!" They begged.

Kalargo laughed uncontrollably. His back ached, abdominal were tight. Bennett had not walked in yet. He had the office on their knees begging for him to stop.

"Just wait till he gets here, he'll tell you." He wipes his eyes with his shirt. "I swear he will tell you the same story. Trust me, I'm not lying." Two of his workers rolled off the couch, they held their sides and tears.

"No more..." they begged. "...you are killing me!" he choked and tried to catch his breath.

Suddenly, Bennett entered the office, and then there was silence, but he could hear the moans of them trying to hold back their laughter. Their faces were filled with this balloon expression of being under pressure.

He looked around the office, and he looked at Kalargo. He shook his head because he couldn't hold water. He knew the joke had to be on him. The office exploded with laughter.

"Ahhh..." he pointed at him, "...you were telling them about my fat girlfriend?" He shook his head.

A voice from behind, "It's true!" and curled over to the floor.

"Hey, hey…" He raised his hand to defend himself, "…I can't help that I like big bitches, fat girls, if she's not over two hundred fifty pounds of good loving, she is too small." He tried to explain his desire for big gals.

"Man, one day one of them whales is going to hurt your tall skinny ass!" Steve said.

He shook his head and pointed his finger at him, "This one already did."
They fell out with laughter.

He walked over and put his diet coke on the desk. "Wait. Let me tell you how it really happened." He began to tell his side of the story.

"Oh shiiit…" Kevin said.

"It'll be my pleasure; God knows what he told you guys." He looked at Kalargo.

"One day I was riding, minding my own business, my mind was not thinking about any fat bitches, low and behold, I needed some smokes. So, I pulled into the convenient store, you know the one on Taano ave and Wawa." He took a sip of his diet coke.

"Now on my way out, I see a crowd of people looking down the street." He pointed in the direction with his hand.

"At first I didn't pay it any mind, but after cranking the car and pulling out of the parking lot." He shook his head in disgust.

"I'll be God damn if I didn't see this huge fat bitch, just ah running down the street, right. Now…" His eyes open wide; he used his hands to form the shape of this huge whale, and his hands were not close together either.

"She passed me. Till this day, I never heard of a…" he was lost for words. "Something as big…I mean elephants don't run this fast." The office begged him to stop.

"Now she already caught my eye with her size, right? But she had the God damn nerve to have a hot pink mini skirt on, legs and all that ass…" his lips curled up bent crooked. "…bounced around, shit no lie. I got excited as hell." He jumped up and down as they burst into laughter. His eyes became tearful.

"Now this bitch running down the street with a jar of damn pickles!" he shook his head wildly, "and it had no top on it! The juice was going everywhere, all on her face, and her clothes." He started to laugh, "Imagine Carl Lewis running the fifty yard dash, now put him in a hippo outfit with a jar of pickles underneath his arms." He tried to hold his composure. He leaned forward.

"And not one pickle came out that jar, not one!" He held his index finger up, took a deep breath and continued.

"She crossed the street going towards that run down gas station. Man… she fell down, bruised her knees, and elbows, but she didn't lose a pickle!" He took another sip of his diet coke. He stood there biting his bottom lip. He was really into telling his version of the story.

"I paused for a moment…I said to myself." He held his left hand across his heart and right hand over his mouth. "Look, just look at my bitch run! Go girl, go!

That's my bitch right there…" He pointed at the wall. He was so excited. "Man I got to have her!"

"So she ran into the men's room, it was dirty, nasty, floor was wet, and the smell was like no other…" before he finished.

Kalargo's cell phone rang; he walked out of the office to avoid the loud laughter.

Bennett continued, "…now this bathroom had me holding my breath…" he deepens his voice, "…but I entered anyway!"

"This bathroom had writing on the walls, mirrors, like call Candy for free blow jobs, and Kitty Kat Pat has no pussy lips." His entire body shook like he was disgusted.

"But…" he held a hand up and changed his voice to this deep Lion King, "I entered anyway!" he lowered his head like he really meant business.

"So I finally saw her, breathing hard as she sat on the wet floor. God knows what was down there before she got there. I looked at this sexy wounded whale." He raised his eyebrows, "Well, I am the eyes of the beholder. I asked her, What the hell are you doing?!" he held his hands over his mouth as if he was really in the bathroom. He spoke threw his mouth due to his thumb and index closing off his nose.

"We looked at each other with this frantic look on our faces. Now, she had these beautiful Asian eyes, soft smooth skin, not one pimple, her hair was long and wavy. She had blonde streaks. Now her breast had to be in the triple D's. I saw that she was nervous, but it was a moment of love at first sight. Do you guys believe in love at first sight?"

They grinned, wiped their tears, and held their abdominals.

"She sat there in the corner behind the toilet with her hand in the pickle jar. Her wide back spread out like heavy wings on a fat angel. Her knees were pulled inward touching her chest. I will not…" the following words he stressed. "…I will not." He twisted his neck and pointed his finger.

"Tell you how turned on I was when I couldn't see her panties due to all of that fat." He smiled and they laughed.

"I…" he held his right hand up to God. "…I love fat bitches. I am a sucker for them." He paused. "I could not see her panties because her fat was just… everywhere. I just knew that she was for me." He licked his chops.

"Guess what she asked me?" he looked around the room.

"What!" Steve boldly asked.

"She bit down on a pickle, and said…" He looked sad when he got to this part of the story. "…did anybody else see me come in here? It's my third strike, I can't get caught."

She had her mouth filled with pickle and talking at the same time. He tossed the empty soda can in the trash like he was talking about the world coming to an end.

"Fellas…I have had at least five beautiful slim women in my life." He cleared his chest of phlegm and swallowed. "Now, don't look at me like I'm sick, but there is nothing like licking that sweaty salty taste that only sit between the fat of a big woman." He held his tongue out with his eyes closed like a sick Lion that have not eating in forty five days. He gave everyone in the office chills and creeps. He made their skin crawl as they fell back with disgusting looks on their faces.

"And you know what? That was five years ago." He pulled out a resent picture of her.

"What!" Steve yelled out.

"No way, can't be her?" Damion said.

For the first time, Bennett looked disgusted, sad; he shook his head, "Yep, that's her."

A voice said, "She is gorgeous. What the hell happened?"

Bennett snatched his photo and shoved it back into his wallet with anger. "What happened? Shit... this bitch started exercising, going on this..." he made this strange facial expression. "Damn diet!"

He slammed his fist into his left hand, "Can you believe the audacity, now she wanted to go on a fucken diet." He shook his head.

Steve stood up, "What a damn minute. You are saying that you are pissed that she lost the weight?"

He grunted and sighed, he rigorously rubbed his hands through his hair. "Guys..." he looked like a poor wounded hyena. "...I pray, I pray to five different Gods..." he started counting with his thumb to his pinky finger, "...to please bring my fat bitch back home." The office filled with laughter.

"No, I am serious, I want my…" He held his hands up in front of him, "…everything about her, the roundness, gone! Big BREAST, GONE! Her ass, GONE! You could just say my dream bitch, GONE!" he tossed his right hand over his shoulder.

"So why haven't you left her yet?" a new guy asked.

"We've been through so much together, most of all, I love her." He walked over to the shelf behind Kalargo's desk and pulled out a magazine. She was on the cover. "I am so proud of her. I…" He was interrupted.

The door opened. "Bennett… I need to talk to you." Kalargo nodded his head to talk with him in private.

*   *   *

Later that night he called Jamie.

"Jamie, what are you doing?"

She was happy to hear from him.

"I need to talk to you. Are you able to come over?" He could not find an easy way to tell her.

"Of course… you sound a little down. Are you ok?" her voice was concerned.

He pulled the cellular away from his ear and sighed with a frustrated expression. "Oh no I am good, just wanted to talk to you, spend a little time together. I'll be here when you arrive; just drive on in, the gate will be open."

After she arrived, he told her he was going on a

business trip that will last two months. He explained how he wanted her to run the gym while he was gone. He had already told his staff that she would be in charge with the help of one of his employees. He also wanted her to check the mail box, make sure the landscapers cut the grass and most importantly to feed the fish. She sat there on the edge of the bed like she had seen a ghost.

"But, when do you have to leave?" she asked with a childish look, reached for his hand and held it tight. She kissed his hand and rubbed it across her face to wipe her tears.

"In six hours." He rubbed his hands through her hair,

Her eyes filled with tears. "You have to… so soon?"She looked in the corner of the room and saw that his carryon bag filled, ready and waiting.

"Oh my God Kalargo, I did not know you would have to go so soon." She stood up on her tip toes and locked her lips on his like a kissing fish. He slowly moved his lips to her eye brows. He held her face in his palms and placed his forehead on hers, "I will miss you."

"Are you going to call me?" she asked.

"Of course I will, every chance I get, I will call you…" he whispered to her ear.

"So that means I can call you?" she waited for him to say yes.

"Yes…" He wrapped his arms around her enter locked his fingers. "…I will have a global phone with me." He sighed. Their French kiss followed with a round of passionate love.

Chapter 11

Seoul, South Korea

Na Min sat at the dinner table resting his left elbow, and holding his reading glasses to his mouth. His wife cooked, and prepared their food. The house smelt like rice and chicken, the Puerto Rican dish that they loved. He had returned from Hawaii the day before and the pressure from the North Koreans to send Kalargo to kill the General, weighed heavy on his mind. He knew that he was more than capable of this mission, but anything can happen and that's what concerned him. He also thought about the damage he has done over the years by giving the North Koreans Top Secret information, it looked like his retirement was his only way out.

He never thought he would ever betray his country, but greed took him under at a time when he was vulnerable, weak, and hurt. In Thailand, he saw how fellow service men smuggled heroin on military planes, not I he had told himself. But this was no different, he felt. May be if he had said something, perhaps all of this could have turned out differently. He shook his head and thought if he had a chance to do it all over again.

He would do it all different. All the money in the world could not replace the pride he had. He rubbed his right hand across his heart. He remembered when he used to pledge to the allegiance when he was in high school in Seattle, Washington. Now his heart felt like an over matured rotten mango that had been stepped on, and remained beneath someone's shoe.

His plate was placed in front of him, cranberry juice to

the left. She returned with hers and sat down. She grabbed his hand and they closed their eyes to pray. He had to ask God to forgive him. He could hear his wife's voice as she prayed out loud, beneath his breath he thanked him for every day he had breathed and to forgive him for taking the breath of others. He slowly opened his eyes and realized that she was waiting on him to open his.

"Are you ok?" she sipped her cranberry juice.

He drove the fork into the yellow rice, "Yeah of course, este es bien." He closed his eyes and chewed on his food.

"Oh you are practicing your Spanish?" They laughed, held hands and kissed.

"One of these months we should fly over to Puerto Rico." He said.

She looked at him and smiled. "Now that sounds like a good idea."

"How is the weather in two months?" he asked her.

"Are you serious?" she was happy. "It's gorgeous…" she tried to continue.

"Now don't quote me, it's just a thought." He put another fork full in his mouth and they enjoyed their dinner as they talked about the Caribbean Islands.

Later that night they cuddle in bed, and watched American TV. He slowly closed his eyes and daydreamed.

It was 1979 Osan, South Korea, in the middle of winter. The door opened and the sound of the blistering wind that blew snowflakes behind Agent Bradley was silenced when the door slammed shut. He stomped his feet, and brushed off the snowflakes that covered his walnut mink trench coat. He snatched off his gloves and looked Na Min dead in his eyes. The sound of the burning wood in the fire place, the smell of it lingered the safe house that was fifteen miles outside the city, and three hours from North Korea.

He sat at the dinner table lighting his tobacco pipe. He wore a caramel thick wool turtle neck sweater, a pair of blue jeans with three pair of long johns beneath them. His beard was a six months of not shaving.

"I thought we were partners?" Bradley threw his gloves on the table and walked over to him in a disturbing manner. He planted the palm of his hands on the dinner table.

Na Min expressed no emotions, and took a drag from his cigar and allowed his smoke to rise in his face.

"What are you talking about?" NaMin looked at him.

"Na Min, what's going on man? We have known each for a long time, and I know when things are not right." Bradley said.

He stood up from the table and grabbed his coat, gloves, and hat that covered his ears. "I told you last week that the drop spot had changed. Did you follow the signs?" Na Min said.

"What signs? You did not tell me about any signs!" Bradley looked confused.

Na Min sighed and knew it was time to get this over with. His pain of broken trust was up to his throat. No matter how he tried to forgive and forget, his voice had begun to gnaw at him like maggots. He kept his furious temper in control.

"Let's go, grabbed your belongings, I guess I have to show you these signs in person." Na Min exhaled his smoke through his nostrils like a mad bull.

They left the house and drove forty five minutes north of the safe house. The weather had worsened; the ground was covered with four feet of snow. The heat in the car was on full blast.

"No wonder you can't see the signs, they are covered by the snow." The chit chat continued, "You make a left turn here." He parked the car and they both got out. There was an old farm house that had not been lived in for five years or more. They walked behind the barn to search for documents. Bradley stopped; he saw a hole that was six feet deep with a small amount of snow in it. He turned around and Na Min had his .45 caliber in his face.

"What the hell are you doing? Are you crazy?" The look on his face was of shock.

Na Min waved the gun at him. "I trusted you." He looked at him. He just had to say these final words. He sighed deeply. "I've been trying to hold this deep anger in for too long."

"But..." Bradley tried to speak.

"Shut up! I don't want to hear it. You destroyed everything I had planned. I was happy. You took away the one thing that I had pride in. Do you know how important family is?" He backed away from him. The wind had reduced their body temperatures. Their faces and toes were going numb, and the feeling of being in the middle of nowhere worried him. He let out visible thick breath from his nose and mouth.

"Na Min…" He held up his hands, and swallowed his saliva, "…relax ok, we can talk this out. We… don't have to do this." He begged him.

He raised his voice, "You think I did not know!?" He gritted his teeth with frustration. He tried to walk away from the grave. The sound of the gun went off.

"Don't move! You really think I don't know? Who you think requested for you to get transferred for duty. Me! I wanted you here. I wanted you! I have tried to get you here for six months. You were denied duty in South America because of me!" he talked and Bradley looked down at the grave.

"Listen, what are you talking about? Are you losing your mind?" The gun went off again, he fell. "Ouch, ahh…" he grabbed his left leg and screamed, "…ass hole…"

He shot him again in the other leg.

"You still want to pretend you don't know what this is about! She told me everything. Na Min tears fell from his eyes. He had been hurting for so long. He had asked God to forgive him for sleeping with his wife Kandance. He had forgiven his wife, but just could not forgive him. Deep down inside he was so torn apart; his anger of the thoughts was eating him alive.

The sound of his cries, he begged for his life. "Na Min, please. Don't do it."

He put the gun to his own head, but he could not do it.

"Why…" Na Min asked.

"You were never home. She needed someone to be there." He applied pressure to his wounds,

"Get me to a hospital, I am going to die out here."

"Die piss ant. I want you to feel what I have been feeling. I have been holding this shit in for way to long. You will die… slow!"

"You want to know something that has been, well a little TOP SECRET mother fucker?" He cracked a smile, a sarcastic one that did not last long.

"Justin was your…" he pointed the pistol at him. "…son, that's right ass hole." He was starting to feel the chill of winter crawl down his back, numb his ears, and fingers.

Bradley looked at him and before he pulled the trigger he asked him for one favor. He begged him to listen. "What about my daughter? Can you look out for Yuki?" he wanted to be told that he would look out for her. He wanted to hear it from his mouth. "And let her know that her father loved her."

Before he squeezed the trigger, "I'll grant you that. I will take her in as my own and I'll always let her know that you loved her." The three gun shots silenced the farm, the cries, the anger, and the hate.

Na Min opened his eyes, and looked at his wife. She was sound asleep. He crawled out of bed in need of a sleeping pill that had been prescribed to him. He shook his head and swallowed them and fell asleep.

      *   *   *

Philippine training camp

The heat and humidity was like wearing a plastic bag with a hundred insects crawling over him. Kalargo was exhausted, sleepy, hungry, and thirsty. The jungle training was intense. He crawled through muddy wet rain forest where everything imaginable lived. He had crawled for three miles, swim across rivers, swamps, peeled leeches from his back, neck, and stomach like relentless duck tape. He carried a small container of water that he could drink every five hours. He was on very strict water consumption for the entire thirty days he had been there. His urine had to be as pure as possible. This was a three day exercise that required him to survive off of the jungle. He didn't mind taste of snakes, frog, and grass hoppers. They were everywhere and easy to catch, and cook. The grass hoppers were a lot easier to catch and swallow so he would grab them as he made his way through the dense jungle.

He looked up at the night sky and saw how beautiful it was. The stars were so bright. It was his final night of training and he was so close to finishing in a record time. So he pushed on to the finish.

He came from a grassy area on to a road that led him to a waiting jeep. The early morning sun crawled out like it was tired of rising. The fellow waiting for him was sound asleep.

"Good morning." Kalargo said.

The Pilipino rebel was startled that he had arrived so soon. He looked at the stop watch, and pushed the button. He spoke in his dialect and tried to speak English but manage to communicate. "You are past." He said with a smile that had missing, rotten, decayed teeth.

"It's fast, with an f. Fast." He tried to correct him. In the Philippine dialects they pronounce their p's like f's and their f's like p's.

"I am starving." he rubbed his stomach to show him what he was saying.

"Yes." he pointed. "Let go." He cranked the jeep and drove off into the sunrise. He tried talking to the driver, but his English was so horrible. It was like trying to talk to six monkeys that studied Rosetta Stone course. So he gave up the conversation and let the driver talk to himself. He inhaled his arm pit of his shirt and frowned, in need of a shower, and a good night sleep.

After breakfast he did his final urine test. He was pissing water by now. He held it up, "Now that is clean." He smiled and handed it to the doctor, Now I can have a diet coke?" He asked the doctor.

The short Pilipino doctor tightens the lid on the cap and said, "No your urine has to maintain clarity for drinking, you can't drink the water there. You will have to drink your own urine if clean water is not available."

He turned around and gave him a plastic bag. "These are your furipiers." They looked like small tubular sugar packages. He opened the plastic bag noticed the different flavors.

"These are to kill the taste in your urine. These…" He pulled one from the bag and to show him. "…I recommend that you start with the lemon flavor first." The doctor said.

Kalargo stood up and walked towards the door. "Doctor… I don't think I could actually drink my own urine." He looked at him.

The doctor smiled, "What do you mean? Your urine has been clean for the last fifteen days, what you think you have been drinking from your canteen? The only difference, the water in your canteen was half and half water, unflavored." He looked him in his eyes like it was no surprise. He pushed up his shoulders like. "I thought you knew already."

Kalargo's jaw dropped and he sighed. "No way…"

"No one told you? Well hey now you know, but make sure…" He held his right index finger up. "…do not lose these. Keep them in this plastic bag. Believe me you will use them sooner or later."

He walked out of the make shift medical office and sighed as he looked up at the sky. A voice came from behind him, "Kalargo… we finally meet." Zang spoke in Korean.

"And who are you?" he asked him in Korean.

He bowed and he did the same. "I am Zang. I came a long way
to meet you." They shook hands.

"I wanted to personally meet you." He directed him to his waiting car. He opened the back door for him and they both chatted as the driver drove around the small terrorist camp.

He had noticed Zang's throat had been slashed and left side of his face had third degree burns from years ago. His hair did a poor job of covering his ear that was reduced to a hole on the side of his head. His voice was hard to understand due to his throat being damaged. That made his Korean harder to comprehend.

"I have to apologize for my Korean. I am lacking the practice. Do you speak English?" Zang laughed as his skin tighten. He blushed.

He tried not to stare at his wounds and that hole on the side of his head.

"Kalrago…" He looked at him. "I speak perfect English." He laughed.

"So… in the morning you will be flying out at four am." He reached in his coat pocket and gave him all the documents that he would need. "Airline tickets, new passport from Canada…driver can you lower the air condition?"

"Yes Mr. Zang." The driver replied.

"When you arrive to Afghanistan, you will change planes to a noncommercial plane to a humanitarian flight to a country in Africa and then you parachute into the Gambia. All of your equipment will be parachuted along with you. Do you have any questions?"

He held the documents in his hand. He read the name on the Canadian driver license. He sighed. He noticed that the airline tickets were purchase through WORLDBRIDGETAVEL.COM.

"Well I guess I don't have any questions. Phone… Can I use your phone?" Kalargo asked.

Zang hesitated. "Well due to security reasons…" He sighed.
He spoke before he did.

"I understand. Everything is a security reason." Kalargo tapped the documents on his thigh. Moments later they pulled up in front of his living quarters.

"Kalargo, I want to wish you good luck and a safe return." They shook hands and he exited the car.

*   *   *

Gambia, Africa

General Kakambo Twigani stood 5'8, hundred eighty pounds, dark complexion and short Afro. His hair looked pushed back like an unwanted hat. At the age of forty two, he became the General of the Gambian Army while his older brother sat on the throne as King.

Their family has ruled the Gambia for more than eighty years. The General smoked Cuban cigars back to back. He always released his smoke through his wide nose like a bull, wore pressed olive green camouflage, and maintained spit shined boots.

He had lost a lot of soldiers and desperately wanted to know who was behind the supplying of the enemy troops. He gave orders to kill any rebel fighter, and take no prisoners. Gambia was in chaos. He chopped a father's head off because his son did not know his name. He felt that if his son did not know who he was. His father had to be a rebel.

"General!" an officer entered his office standing at attention with good news to report. He saluted the General. After returning his salute, he approached his desk.

The General converted an abandoned church that was riddled with bullet holes into his headquarters. His office was located in the basement. The paint on the walls had pealed and distorted the faces of the painted angels. His photo of him in his younger days hung behind him. The dust blanked the cracked concrete floor; Cuban cigar smoke lingered and found its way out every time the door opened.

"We have gained control of the cities of Kaba, Gubio, and Mostiwa." the officer said. The entire church vibrated after a bomb exploded, dust floated from the ceiling.

General Twigani removed his cigar from his mouth with his right hand. He stood with excitement. "Yes!" He walked around the small four legged table and stood in front of the map that hung on the wall. He exhaled smoke from his nose and pointed to the map with his cigar between his fingers.

"We have to have this town back." He said with his back facing the officer. He spoke about his home town.

"What town is that?" the officer walked over and stood next to him.

"The town of Magbigan." He took a long drag as the cherry brighten on the cigar.

Officer Baggihk closed his eyes as the smoke irritated them.

"How's your family doing?" The General asked him.

"Sir its war, they are either dead or relocated to refugee camps."

The General turned around and looked up at the ceiling. "I would consider yourself lucky. The King and I are the only survivors in our family. For our family sake, we must win this war. Don't you agree?" He looked at him. He placed red flag thumb tacks on the cities of Kaba, Gubio, and Mostiwa.

"Of course."

Dust floated from the ceiling again. "How hard can it be to find the bastards that's bombing the runway?" before the officer could respond.

"Yes, we have control of the airport, but what good is it if we can't land on the damn thing." His cigar was short and midget like compared to a new one.

"I have a question for you, do you know who's supplying these rebels?" the General walked over to his desk and put the cigar out in the ash tray.

"You will be the first to know." He said.

"Coffee?" He offered the officer as he poured his own.

"No sir. I have work to do. Thanks anyway." He saluted the General, "Permission to leave sir?"

The General returned his salute and the officer walked out the office, dust floated from the ceiling, he looked up and sighed.

Chapter 12

Seoul, South Korea

Yuki lay next to Mugumbi with tears slowly falling sideways towards her ear. His right leg crossed her legs as he lay asleep. They both snuggle under a purple silk comforter that had small designs of gold umbrellas. She opened her blurry wet eyes to see the white carpeted bedroom.

She saw herself in the mirrored wall across from the bed. The sound of the water bed occasionally rippled. She turned over to her left side and looked at the clock. She closed her eyes and tried not to think of her biological father, CIA agent Bradley.

Yuki's mother died when she was born. Her father was the best thing she ever had. She frequently dreamed of her father's funeral, and how Na Min walked her up to his casket. He held her hand and picked her up as they got closer. She slowly fell back to sleep under Mugumbi's arms.

*　　　　　*　　　　　*

The smell of blueberry candle danced Na Min's newly decorated office. The leather cream sofa against the far wall with an oil based painting of him. He sat there with a picture in his left hand of his family, wife, and children.

He removed his reading glasses to wipe a falling tear. Beneath his eyes were puffy and his face had grown wrinkle over the years. He rubbed his forehead with his right hand. He had a receding hair line with a substantial amount of gray hair. But for an old man, he was in good health.

He went into deep thought that took him back thirty years. He was twenty five years old on his first assignment for the CIA in Central America. As an Intelligence officer, it was his duty to train the rebels and interrogate prisoners; all information was directly reported to his senior officer in D.C.

San Salvador was a beautiful country with some of the most gorgeous people of the region. However, it was also a place of many horrors and theses horrors eventually consumed him. Na Min had become a viscous cold blooded killer, blood thirsty was a better way of describing him. His methods of interrogating went from the norm to the extreme, even torture, and death. He had grown accustomed to witnessing, and participating in some of the most horrific tortures to mankind. He was highly recommended for leading all interrogations. He no longer followed the rules of Geneva. He was known to be out of control.

The morning of June 8, four am, he crawled and inched his way between two bushes, with his binoculars to his eyes, the muddy dirt painted his face. He focused in on a communist rebel army camp.

"Let me see what we have here." He whispered out to a San Salvadorian platoon leader.

"Now, if I could find out who is supplying them their weapons?" He sighed and passed the binoculars to the platoon leader. "Look, tell me what you see just passed the tent."

Na Min rolled over to his left. He wore green fatigues and black soldier boots. His uniform had no insignia or country of origin. It took ten days of crossing the jungle. The platoon of novice soldiers were exhausted but under good leadership.

The small camp consisted of approximately forty rebels and lots of supplies. It was imperative that he find out the supply route and supplier.

"Juan, in that tent I believe there are at least twelve soldiers." he reached for the binoculars with his left hand. He slowly pulls a leaf down to get a better view.

"In one hour, we will be able to see better with early morning sunrise." He whispered.

"Na Min, I think it would be better if we call in for an air strike." Juan said.

Na Min sighed, "Just make sure we don't blow everything to pieces, I would like to be able to interrogate someone this time."

"Hey don't blame that last one on me. I had a new radioman. He gave the coordinates." Juan explained.

"Well either the radioman could not read your writing or you gave him the wrong coordinates. Either way, we can't afford to not get a lead on this supply trail. I mean just imagine how far we have come. If we blow this, I can truly say your country will be at civil war for many years to come." he looked at him, and patted him on the shoulder.

"It would be big news if the Russians are supplying but even worse, Fidel." Carlos said and slapped the back of his neck to kill a mosquito.

"It's all the same, If the Cubans or the Russians. Everybody knows who backs Cuba, but to have someone to point the finger would make it a lot easier." Na Min said.

Juan approached three of his soldiers, "Listen, in one hour, Jose take seven men and set up a perimeter on the left flank." He said as he reached deep into his shirt to pull out a map.

"Gomez, take six of your guys just on the right flank." He pulled his flash light out and held it between his teeth to keep a steady aim on the map. He closely examined the map to coordinate the air strike. "Now Gomez, take these, you see the tent right there?"

"Si senor." he peered through the binoculars, "Na Min believes the most important people in the camp are there, so you know what that mean?"

Gomez used his arm sleeve to wipe his sweat from his forehead and nose. "Si yo se que debo de hacer." He tried to speak his English, "Shoot for legs, no kill." He pointed at Carlos's legs.

Na Min sat beneath a tree thinking his plan through. He hoped to have at least five prisoners to interrogate. Juan came from behind; "Smokes?" he pulled one from the pack and Juan lit them both.

"In fifteen minutes…" He looked at his watch and let out a huge puff of smoke. "Gomez and Jose will have their teams in
position."

After the air strike the smell of burning flesh, rubber, and debris filled the air. The injured can be heard, but slowly and quietly dying off. His special team of four waited for the green light that everything was secured. The crackle sound that came over the radio said, "Todo bien, todo bien, operacion exito."

"OK boys and girls let's see what we have here to work with." Na Min said to his team.

They used their machetes to cut through the three hundred feet of dense jungle and down the slope that led them to the camp. He patiently walked through the camp using his feet and occasionally is hands to turn bodies over.

"Hmmm…" he mumbled with the tip of the cigarette but barely hanging between his lips. Juan came over with excitement, jumping over debris and bodies.

"Senor, we have fifteen prisoners for interrogation." He sighed and wiped his sweat from his forehead. His armpits were wet and his American m-16 was strapped around his back.

"Well, let's get this party started." he said with confidence, "If anyone knows anything, we'll get it out of them." He took a deep drag from his cigarette.

"Juan, set up a make shift tent here and I want you to put the prisoners…" he pointed. "… there."

He immediately started snapping his fingers and yelling in Spanish.

"Na Min, one of my soldiers found some documents-you might be interested in." He told him as he pulled out his box of cigarettes from his top left pocket.

The young soldier gave the documents to him. He looked no older than sixteen years old. He looked over the papers.

"Now this…" he waved the papers above his right shoulder. "…is interesting." He stuffed the papers in his right side pants pocket. "Where are these so call prisoners?"

They brought fifteen guys, some were tied, and others too wounded to tie up. They all looked like they wished they were dead. Na Min slowly walked through them, looking at each one. He finally made his decision.

"Him!" he pointed.

The prisoner eyes opened wide and the fear on his face closed his mouth with a wrinkle pout. A soldier picked him up by the back of his shirt collar and practically dragged him to the front of the group.

"Juan, I want you to translate for me. Tell the rest of them that I am here for information only. They can make it easy or hard. I have all day, but I won't spend all day asking the same questions. I personally don't…" He kind of waved his hands in the air with a sarcastic grin, "…have that kind of all day patients. However, there will be an award for cooperating."

Juan could be heard translating every word like a bilingual parrot. He continued, and the prisoners paid close attention as Na Min walked towards his first prisoner. He used his right thumb to close off right nostril, blew mucous from his nose, and wiped his hand on the back of his pants.

"Are you a talker?" He waited for a response, "Tommy, bring me that can of gas."

He was cold hearted, by now he had over forty two murders under his belt. In a normal world he would be considered a serial killer, but in this situation, location, circumstances, he is the God of information extraction, but an example always had to set, and unfortunately. Any many miny moe either way somebody will have to die first.

The soldier started speaking Spanish. As far as he was concerned, he had no real use for him. He knew this poor peasant was worthless. He had chosen him just to kill. He was no more than an insect to him, someone to torture to get the others ready to talk. He knew they'll be begging to talk first.

He looked in the eyes of the others and saw the fear in their eyes, but it was the same fear that he had seen before, not fearful enough. Some mumbled Spanish reiterate of some sort, others began crying with those senseless crocodiles tears that won't save them. The sound of the match grew the cries wider. Their death was eminent by the hands of a monster. Some looked up like they had an unforgiving God.

"Na Min, I think we can interrogate a different way! This is insane!" Juan spoke out loud.

"You think so!" like a monster on steroids; "I don't have any more patients to dick around with these dirt farmers!" he walked over to him. He put the match to his cigarette and inhaled. He looked at him directly in his eyes.

"These are the same farmers who are resisting and fighting against democracy." With a calm and mellow voice, Na Min blows smoke over his shoulder. He takes a visual survey of Juan's soldiers watching the scene.

He leaned in closer and whispered in his left ear, "Juan don't ever interrupt my God damn interrogation, ever, under any circumstances, claro?" He patted him on the shoulder and smiled at everyone else.

"Si Senor." Juan felt threaten.

Na Min turned around and slowly walked over to the prisoner that was soaked in gasoline. "Juan! Tell these bastards they have two minutes to tell me where and who are supplying them ammo, weapons, and bla bla bla" He pointed his index finger at each of them, with his right boot he pushed a small pile of dirt back and forward.

The early morning sun gave light to the damage to the camp. Most of his soldiers were gathering what they could. His team surrounded the prisoners with an additional soldiers from the platoon watched.

"Translate, if you dirt farmers want to save this poor comrade of yours from burning a painful death..." he inhaled on his cigarette. Juan's voice can be heard translating in the background. Three of the prisoners started saying, "Padre Nuestro que esta en el cielo, santificado sea tu nombre..."

Those that did not have a higher power chose other final words to comfort them.

"Speak your mind to forever hold your peace." he put the cigarette close to the wet prisoner.

The prisoner closed his eyes and screamed, quickly saying the Lord's Prayer, "Padre Nuestro, que esta en el cielo, santificado sea tu nombre..."

Just before he flicked the cigarette, a brave soul yelled out,"Te hablare!"

Na Min quickly pointed him out like God gave him this power to torture human beings. "Take him! Translate! If you lie to me, any of you, I will know!"

The prisoner was dragged across the early morning dark wet dirt with his hands tied in front of him. He begged to spare his life.

"Ask him! Where and who is supplying them?" His voice echoed throughout the camp.

The nearby birds flew away to safety. The sound of a grown men cried, the prisoner was covered in blood, and dirt. He looked malnourished and pitiful. He bowed back and forward, begging and pleading for forgiveness in Spanish.

Juan translated, "He said, 'Please don't kill his brother. He is the last brother that he has." He paused to see how he would respond.

"What does he know about the supplies?!" Na Min demanded.

The prisoner's hands were up to his face begging him like a helpless peon. He crawled towards Carlos. He held on to his left leg like a child that is happy to see their father. Carlos kicked him in the face.

He proceeded towards Na Min like an animal begging for food. He praised and kissed his boots. He snatched his left foot and then his right boot away from his lips. "This is pathetic and depressing. What is he saying? Did he answer my question?"

Juan sighed heavily, with his mouth filled with air. He slowly let it out and shook his head. His five o'clock shadow beard gave him this exhausted look on his face. He didn't want to tell him what he had said.

"What did he say?!" Na Min asked.

"He said he does not know anything about where and how…" He combs his right hand through his hair, "…he is begging you not to kill his brother. They are the last men in their family." He looked up at the sky and rubbed his five o'clock shadow beard.

"Well I can see for myself that he is begging Juan!" Na Min paused. "So nobody knows anything." He walked around the prisoners to come in between the brothers. "I am not here for family counseling, family matters, or any other crap they will try to throw at me. I want facts, info, and what the hell are two brothers doing fighting." He pointed his finger at them both.

"You knew you two were not going to make it…" He cracked an ugly smile at them. He sighed and cleared his throat and tried to spit but it hung from his mouth like a long spaghetti noodle that would not break away. He used his left hand to break it off.

"Juan, tell him for his brother's sake… I won't kill his only brother…" he played with a small pile of dirt with his left boot.

The prisoner became joyful. He crawled over to his brother and put his tied hands around him and cried.

Na Min walked over to them both and pulled out his .45 caliber and shot him. "But, I did not say I would spare you." He said as he stood over them both. The smoke lingered from the barrel. One shot to the chest, and he watched him struggled for his final breathe for four minutes. The brother screamed as his older brother bled to death with his arms around him.

The silence among the prisoners was like they had died, speechless, the fear kept them quiet. Suddenly, three soldiers tried to get away. "Shoot them in the legs! Now I have who I am looking for." He smiled and put his .45 in his holster and fastened the leather strap.

"I want these three separated from each other. Have the rest start digging holes. If they are too injured to dig, kill them!" he yelled out loud, "It was about time we got down to the bottom of this mess. After they dig the holes…" He whispered to Carlos. "… Kill them all."

*   *   *

Six months later
Washington D.C.

"Today is promotion day." Na Min embraced his wife and locked his lips with hers. He rubbed her back and soothed her muscles.

"I am so glad you invited the family to join you. You have no idea how much we have missed you." She told him with her Eskimo kisses.

Kandance remained a stunning blonde for having two kids. She stood 5'9 at a hundred twenty five pounds. She was not bad for an ex model. She thought about going back into the modeling business just to keep her busy. She ran five miles a day and dieted to remain in shape. They met in college in a fitness gym. She was attracted to Asian men as he was attracted to blondes. She set aside her career goals to be with him.

She wore a white blouse and blue jean shorts, her hair pinned up in a bun. She walked across the hotel room, stepped over Cynthia and called for Justin.

"Are you hiding again?" She asked with a smile as she entered the bathroom. From the bathroom her voice can be heard "Honey, maybe we could do this more often…" she looked out from the bathroom door, so happy to be with him. "…you know, travel and meeting you in different locations. That would be nice, right?" She ducked back into the bathroom, grabbed her toothbrush and toothpaste. She walked out with the toothbrush in her mouth.

He knew that would be a security risk. Before he could disappoint her, she said "I know everyone has a job to do…" she stood in front of him, cheerful, and talking with a mouth full of toothpaste, smoothly brushing her teeth.

"But I know the agency, perhaps that would be a risk of security, right?" she asked.

He stood up, "Damn, you are right, but if I could get around it, you bet we all would be in some of the places that I go to."

She returned to rinse her mouth, "And then we could visit all the beautiful cities that you go to."

"Daddy, what time are we leaving?" Cynthia asked. She had been asking to go to the Washington D.C. Zoo every since she saw the hotel pamphlet.

Justin, her younger brother came from under the bed. "Yeah, don't forget parrot jungle."

Cynthia pinched him and said "Parrot Jungle is in Florida."

Justin rubbed his arm with a frown, and begins to cry. She walked over to apologize, but he balled into a fetal position and hid beneath the bed.

"Justin boy, stop crying and be a big boy." Na Min changed his voice to soothe his pain, "Stop letting these girls see you cry." He stood in front of the bed and picked him up, tickled him until he heard him laugh. "You aren't hurt, boy stop playing."

His head peeked through with a big smile. "I love you daddy."

"I love you too." He held him high and bounced him onto the bed.

Then Cynthia jumped on the bed. "Look mommy look."

Kandance smiled, looked at the hotel clock. "OK kids, it's time to go to bed. We have an early wake up call." The laughter that smeared the room settled down.

"Did you put in for the 7 o'clock wakeup call?" Na Min asked.

"No, actually 8 am, did you want 7 am?" she looked at him.

"Hmmm, 8 am is good, ok kids settle down and get ready for bed." He said.

The hotel phone rang. "Yes hello this is Marriott guess services. We are confirming your wake up call for 8 am correct?" before she could respond, "We also would like to offer a full breakfast delivered to your room, free of charge, are you interested?"

"One moment please." She put them on hold.

"Yes we would be interested."

"What time would you want breakfast to be delivered?"

"9 am sharp." She looked at him, he didn't disagree.

"It will be the continental breakfast for a party of four; it comes with a jug of orange juice, milk, and croissants."

"Thank you." Moments later she softly placed the receiver on the phone.

Na Min tossed and turned throughout the night. His sleeping medication kept the nightmares to a minimum. He finally opened his eyes to look at the clock.

"Damn…" he sighed, "…still too early." He rubbed his eyes and cleared his throat. The clock said four thirty am. He twisted his back until his bones crack one after another. He twisted his head to his left and right to crack his neck bones. He stood up and bent down to touch his toes, and forced his forehead to touch his knees.

The room was dark with only the television on. The broadcast had ended and
the sound of static echoed the family suite. He paused and looked at how uncomfortable his son looks as he lay on the bed. He walked over and tucked him neatly, and kissed

him on the forehead and thought of all the freedom that they have. He walked over to the window and pulled the curtain to look from the sixth floor. An inch of snow had fallen over night, and the remaining flurries floated softly. In the distance he could see the white house and Capitol Hill. He closed the curtain and walked into the bathroom and pissed. The sound of falling liquid echoed, until it dripped. He grabbed a small amount of tissue to wipe the toilet seat, and flushed. He looked into the mirror as he washed his hands. He looked at his tattoo of a lion head with torn arm in his mouth. He rubbed it and thought of the day he had it done. He quickly hit the light switch, it brought back to many memories.

He crawled back into bed and held his wife tight, "Honey…" She spoke in a low voice and turned on to her right side. She felt his breath on the back of her neck. His lips nibbled her ear. Her left hand reached behind her buttocks to caress his mighty python. She stroked him until his erection was powerful. His left hand found its way between her legs. Her breathing became heavy as his middle finger groped her lips, pushed her clit to the left, right, and finally snorkeled its way deep in to her wet pawn. She held him as his breathing increased with his heart beat. Suddenly, they stopped and looked across the room.

"They still sleep?" she asked.

"Hmm, yeah." he moved his middle finger faster. She put her left hand to her mouth and licked her palm twice to lubricate her palm.

"Oh my." he said. He penetrated deep and she stroked him faster. He stopped to look at the children. "Still sleep?"

She squeezed his monster tight, gritted her teeth and

threatened him with a horny agitated whispering voice, "If you stop again when I'm ready to cum. I will snatch it off!"

He quickly rotated his index finger across her clit, her back arched. She grabbed the sheets into a bundle. He spoke softly in her ear. "Let's finish this in the bathroom."

She stopped and looked at the kids. They were sound asleep. With a smile she French kissed him and tossed the bed sheets to the floor.

He held his head back and slowly caressed her head. They made passionate love until they could no longer stand. The print of her back smeared the mirror. Their bodies were weak and sweaty. He placed her on the edge of the sink and vacuumed her love pawn dry; her knees trembled as she moaned beneath her breath.

"Quack Quack!" he stepped on a rubber duck as he picked her up and carried her to the bedroom. She held him tight with her arms around his neck; she licked his sweat from his face, and shoved her tongue down his throat. He placed her on the bed and lay next to her naked underneath the sheets. Their heart beats slowly came to a normal strong thump. Their over worked bodies felt heavy, it didn't take them long to fall asleep.

The sunrise eased its way between the curtains and the early wakeup call tortured them. "My God, please answer that."

She picked up the receiver and placed it back down. "Honey, it's time to get up." She said with her thumb and index finger closing his nose. His eyes opened with a moan, and turned over. His right leg hung off the edge of the bed. His right arm lay beneath his body. She embraced him.

"I love you." She said.

He moaned, lifted his head and looked over at the kids. His head fell like a bowling ball into the pillow. "Yeah yeah…" he said in Korean.

Kandance lay across from him. She looked at the kids and turned to him. "Are you ready for round two?"

"Hell no." He mumbled in Korean.

"Oh what does that mean?" She smiled with her right hand beneath the sheets and holding his Johnson. "Look like somebody is ready for round two." She smiled.

"Well in Korean, that means hell no, but you can run my shower for me." He smiled.

She smiled, licked her beautiful lips, and tossed her hair from her face, "Anything for my Emperor."

He watched her sexy ass walk across the room; he smiled and knew that he was the luckiest man alive.

She wakes the kids as he showered; his 1:30 pm meeting with the director of the CIA will be in Langley, Virginia. He had murdered a lot of people to get this information and it has finally paid off. He discovered the North Koreans were supplying the rebels; he had photos, and document to prove it.

"Honey, did you pack my republican tie… you know my favorite red tie with the gold leaves on it?" he asked while he was drying off. He could hear her mumbling, it took her a moment to search the luggage. She sighed in disappointment and knew this was his favorite tie that his father gave him. He always felt like it was his good luck charm. It made him feel confident, and gave him a sense of empowerment.

"Damn, how could I have forgotten it?" She questioned herself, "Honey." She spoke sadly. It didn't sound like she had found it. "I completely forgot it. I swear I took it out of the closet…" She tries to explain before he gets upset. She remembered how he responded the last time he got upset over wasted tooth paste awhile back. She stopped and said no more. It was silent for a moment, she thought quickly, "Hey I'll run down and get another tie."

He walked out of the bathroom, "Don't worry about it. You go ahead get the kids ready and I'll run down to the gift shop to get something." He held the towel around his neck and put his lips on hers. She smiled and sighed.

He arrived to the gift shop in tennis shoes without socks, a thin sweater, and damped hair. He looked desperate to find something. He looked around before asking the salesman.

"Are these the only ties you have?" He asked impatiently.

The salesman frowned "Unfortunately, that's all we have."

He rolled his eyes and headed out the door.

"For your information, there is a store on the corner." He twisted his lips in a girlish manner, and moved his hands like he had a broken wrist. His well manicured glossy nails were moving in every direction. When they finally stopped in the direction of the store, he bolted out of the gift shop saying, "Thanks!"

He found the store to be closed, "No! No! No!" He stood there as the cold air gave him a chill. He danced a little to keep warm. He held his hands in front of his mouth to warm them. He looked up at the sky as the snowflakes fall. Suddenly he saw a sales woman pass, "Hey!" He tapped on the glass door and frantically pointed at his watch.

"What time you open?" He could feel his toes starting to get cold.

She walked over to the door and smiled; one of those pseudo retail smiles. "Fifteen minutes!" she yelled through the glass doors and pointed at the clock on the wall.

He shivered and lowered his head, "I… do I look like I can wait fifteen more minutes?"

She thought he was cute, and desperate to get inside from the elements. She looked at her watch and the clock on the wall, "You have to wait fifteen more minutes." She walked away.

He pulled his badge and tapped it hard on the glass. He was frustrated. She turned around, but the badge changed her attitude. She looked at him and felt sorry for him. She threw up both of her hands and said, "The key."

She returned a couple of seconds later, bent down like a lady with her knees together and upper body twisted to accommodate her position.

Before she turned the key she asked, "Let me see that badge again… I know a fake one when I see one." The sound of the key unlocked the door. The cold air rushed in and the sound of the early morning commute filtered into the store.

"Oh thank you so much." He stood there to brush off the snow flakes, and tried to get comfortable in the heated store.

"What are you doing without a coat?" the saleswoman asked.

He interrupted her, "I need a tie...prefer red." He said with a gesture of urgency. He still held his hands to his mouth.

She felt ignored. "Yes we have some blue ties."

"You have no idea how important this is to me. I thank you from the bottom of my heart." He followed her toward the suites and ties.

The saleswoman was a beautiful 5'6, dark eyed, curly haired Puerto Rican, shape was to die for and her accent was a sniper in the bush and she admired him for some reason.

"I take it you have an important meeting you have to go to?" she asked cunningly as she flirted.

He was so into finding the perfect tie. He hadn't noticed her gestures. "What about these ties?"

"Is that... well that's not the only tie you have... is it?" He impatiently searched for another suitable tie.

He frantically looked at his watch, "Damn! You..."

"Listen..." she interrupted him. "Hey I have more ties in the back that I guarantee you would not walk out of here without."

Moments later she returned with an arm filled with some of the most beautiful ties in the world. "Now here are…" she was interrupted.

"You have to help me. My wife shop for my ties…" he said carefully holding two ties in the air for comparison.

She smirked and picked out the most expensive tie. Her attitude changed from a flirting to a disappointed one, voice became tolerating than a helping one.

"Well…" she picked out a blue tie, "…this is your tie that you have to buy. It goes with all suits. The colors that twine in between…"

He stopped her. "Excuse me, I am so sorry, but I have to really be somewhere. Just charge it to my credit card." He put his credit card on the glass counter.

"Do you have I.D.?" she asked.

He showed her his C.I.A. badge and identification. "Do you have state I.D.?"

He impatiently reached for his wallet, "Here!" He rudely put it on the glass instead of her hand and sighed with frustration.

She look at it, compared the two.

He combed his fingers through his jet black hair and rolled his eyes. "Aah…how much is it?"

She pulled the tag from the back of the tie and cleared her throat, "Eight hundred dollars and forty three cents." She frowned and he almost past out.

"What! Eight hundred dollars and forty three cents." he

looked at the clock. "This is not the cheapest tie you have!" He panicked as he almost pulled his hair out.

"Well... you did ask for red..." she pushed her lips upward and forced herself to smile. "And this is the last tie that we have.", before she could say another word.

"Just charge it." He told himself that he would most definitely bring it back. He shook his head as the machine made all kind of noise as it printed the receipt. He wanted to reach over and choke this bitch, but it was not her fault, beside he had just noticed how cute her accent was. She was beautiful, make up was flawless, teeth were pearly white; she used her right index to specifically scratch in one spot of her scalp.

She held his credit card closer to her face to read his name, "Mr. Choi." He nodded his head.

"Not many people can pronounce it." He looked at her name tag and said her name with the proper Spanish accent.

She was shocked, "wow..."

He stopped her before she could ask. "It's a good chance that I speak Spanish better than you."

She handed him his credit card and I.D. with his bag with the tie in it. He quickly said his good bye and dashed out of the store with his credit card and receipt between his lips. A snow flake touched his eyebrow, the cold winter elements rushed him as he hurried back to the hotel, being occupied with putting everything back in his wallet and the sound of the snow crunched after every step. Thinking it was dumb of him to leave without a jacket. He wanted to make it back to eat breakfast with his family, something he had not done in three years.

Kandance heard a knock at the door, "Who is it?" She walked towards the door.

"It's room service."

The kids got excited, "Ok kids, it's time to eat breakfast."

"Where is daddy? Cynthia asked.

"He should be back soon."

Kandance opened the door, "Good morning."

The waiter pushed the cart in to the room, "You have to sign here Ma'am." He gave her the bill.

"Is that it?"she asked.

"Yes Ma'am, enjoy." She gave him a tip and closed the door behind him.

"OK Justin!" she arranged the table, "Come have a sit at the table." She pushed the cart and the table closer to the window as they gathered around as she opened the curtains.

"Mommy can I have extra bacon?" Cynthia asked.

Down below, Na Min was a hundred feet from the entrance to the Marriott. Suddenly, the explosion vibrated the surrounding buildings, shattered windows across the street. He fell to his knees as debris of glass and brick hit him. The people on the street panicked; nearby car alarms sounded, people ran for their lives.

He stood and wiped his eyes and noticed he was

bleeding. He looked up at the hotel and saw that it was his hotel room that had exploded. He screamed.

"Noooo!" he looked on the ground and saw one of his son's shoes. He folded. "Nooooo!" he cried. The smoke from the hotel burned. He looked around and ran to his daughter. He was having a difficult time swallowing his pain. He held her, and cried. She was dead. She was missing an arm and a leg.

"Cynthia! Cynthia!" he held her close. He tried mouth to mouth resuscitation. She was gone. He screamed to the top of his lungs, "Why!" He yelled in Korean.

"Kandance! Justin!" He stood up and frantically searched. He was covered in his daughter's blood.

His tears fell and choked him. His wife lay on top of the hood of a taxi. He ran over to her with a loss for words. He touched her, her eyes opened. "Help is on the way!"

She cried and held him while she went into shock. He was so nervous; he couldn't think straight. Her legs were gone and blood pumped out. He carried her from the hood of the taxi to the sidewalk.

She grabbed him, "Justin!" She tried to scream. Her voice was cracked and low. She grabbed her chest and frowned. She had a puncture wound to her lungs. "Justin… save my boy!" she pointed.

He looked in the direction that she pointed. He ran over, but it was too late. "Justin! Don't you die on me! No!" he picked him up and carried him to his mother. He looked fine, but he had a puncture wound to his heart.

"Cynthia!?" she asked.

He cried as the sirens got closer. She took her last breath. Justin died moments later, no longer bothered by the cold winter morning. His anger heated him.
He slammed his fist on to the sidewalk until his knuckles bled. He rested on his knees; he slowly forced his hands to come to his face.

"Our father ..." he prayed for the first time in five years. He fell forward as he mumbled the Lord's Prayer out of his mouth. He collapsed to the side walk, curled like an infant; the love of his life was snatched from him. He had wished he had died. He never recovered mentally from this lost.

He sat there at his desk holding a family photo. His wet eyes were evidence that he could not hide from his current wife; she walked into his office.

"Honey, are you ok?" She stood at the door.

"Yeah." He picked up his glass of Genifer and took a sip and sighed. She knew there were times he would go through a moment of depression, especially, when he thought about his kids, and she was unable to bare any. She walked over and kissed him on the lips. He looked at the photo of Kalargo when he was fourteen in his martial art class. He was so proud of him, and most of all, that he had adopted him.

They cut the lights out and walked out of the office.

Chapter 13

Seoul, South Korea

One year had passed after the hotel bombing, "Did you meet your contact? He asked.

Bradley sighed, scratched his eyebrow, he exhaled the visible hot breath from his mouth and nose. His scarf was wrapped around his neck. He stomped his feet and rubbed his hands. It was very cold; they both looked like Michelin men under their clothes. He blew on his hands to keep them warm. He opened the back door of the fish market and Agent Bradley followed.

Agent Bradley was born Korean American working deep cover in South Korea and North Korea as a C.I.A. operative. He looked one hundred percent Korean and spoke their language with no foreign accent. Both of his parents were born in South Korea and he had lived in Seoul, South Korea until the age of fourteen.

He was very comfortable being in his home country, among his family helped blend him in very well. But he and his daughter lived in the United States. He was older than Na Min, but he looked up to him like a hero. He had heard of the Central America interrogations. He felt like he was working with a legend.

The 10 degree below zero weather chilled them to their bones. They sighed after the door was closed and stood there and let the heat absorb their faces before they stomped the ice from their boots.

He looked at him with this stupid look on his face before he smiled. "Yes!" he said with an excited but low tone of voice.

"I have…" he pulled him aside and reached in his pocket. "He showed him a roll of film. "Launch pads, bases, missile storage, and…" they quickly changed the subject as a worker walked passed them. He slowly slid the roll of film back into his pocket. They took their coats off and hung them on the coat hooks.

"Are you guys working or chatting for a pay check?" the supervisor asked them both.

They remained in character, "We work for our checks boss!"

"I'll believe it when I see it."

"You are on table one and Na Min take table three, Kim can't make it today." Their supervisor walked away.

Before they separated Bradley pulled him by his shirt and whispered, "Our tunnels are complete; we can go in to the north whenever we want now."

A loud voice in Korean came over the loud speaker, "Hey we need more eel head, and octopus heart!"

"Right on it!" He yelled back, smiled and sighed at his flawless Korean.

"Yeah and guess what..." he leaned towards him, looked away a moment. Na Min's butcher knife cut open a baby octopus in half. He frowned and could not stand his deep cover assignment.

"They are making a submarine that carry nukes." They

both chopped up eels and octopus. The smell of the sea no longer bothered them.

"We need to get over there and take photos." Na Min said.

Bradley pulled out a small folded paper with his finger tips, carefully to not get blood on it. "Check this out." he raised his eyebrows. "Wow, tell me this is not what I think it is?" he quickly shoved it in his back pocket."Six months, it will be completed."

"How did you get this?" Na Min looked at him strangely. He always tried to impress him; he knew it would do exactly that and also bring him closer to his death.

"Another thing, this job has to go!" he pointed his long pointy knife at him.He laughed, "This is where I get all of my drops."

"Eel, octopus ready!" Na Min said.

"If it's not broke, don't fix it." Bradley looked at him.

"Whale eyes, ready!" Bradley said.

The sound of their stainless steel knives can be heard chopping away.

"This needs to be cut in smaller portions!" the head fisherman
said. They looked at each other, and then at the packaged fish.

"This is it." they both reached for it. Bradley grabbed it first. They looked around the kitchen suspiciously. He ran his hand in between the guts of this huge eel. He felt something.

"Yes, this is it." he pulled out a roll of film that had been wrapped in plastic. Bradley had this nervous feeling that he had never felt before.

Na Min wiped his forehead with the inside of his sweaty forearm. He held his butcher knife in his left hand. They smiled.

"Good work. Damn good work, but I could have done it without..." he kind of nodded his head to the left. "...may be hurting someone." They both smiled.

Six months later

"This is good, look at this." Na Min looked at the negative at an angle above his head; holding it between his finger tips.

"Beautiful. They are going to slobber all over these." Bradley said.

Their safe house was close to the DMZ (demilitarize zone).

The Korean War never really ended between the south and the north. For almost twenty years they have been at war. But not a bullet has been fired. The American and South Koreans stand guard all day, every day. It is so intense around the DMZ, no one is allowed to smile, show fear, or help the enemy.

The white paint that separates the south from the north is twelve inches in width. The soldiers are always at attention or in the ready position.

"Yep, this is definitely what they are looking for." he said as he held another negative towards the ceiling.

"OK tomorrow would be a good time to go to Seoul." Bradley said.

"You want me to make reservations?" Na Min asked.

"Yes." He holds a negative in each hand up to the light.

The following day
Seoul, South Korea

"Yes, how can I help you?" a beautiful Korean asked.

"Hmm, yes we have two rooms reserved for five nights." the sound of the computer keys tapped away.

"Do you have identification?" she smiled, her straight black hair passed her elbows, no cleavage, but her blue suit fitted her well.

She turned away to code their room keys. Her calves were thick, and hips flat.

"OK gentlemen, your rooms are across from one another. If you need any assistance dial seven, for room service dial eight, and for emergencies dial nine." she pushed the keys across the counter. She ripped the receipt from the printer.

"And you must sign... here, and here." she pointed at both of the receipts.

Bradley looked at his watch, "Still early, first thing first, I'll run over to the base..." he touched his watch.

"I'll find Mr. Bonjivich to develop these negs."

"We'll meet back here at nineteen hundred hour." they both agreed and separated to their rooms.

1830 hundred hours

Na Min returned early, slowly slid in his key, the light blinked, the sound of the lock unlocked. He struggled to retrieve his key for a moment. The door opened. The beige carpet matched the bed spread and the contrast of wallpaper said a lot about the interior designer. He had to be drunk or blind, but the hotel was super clean, and dated.

He rushed toward the bathroom as he begin to remove some of his clothes, unbuckle his pants; he passed the television, queen size bed, office desk, and the old rusty iron heater. He thought he would have gotten down to the third layer of clothes by now.

"God damn it!" He danced, wiggled his way around the bathroom floor, still not ready, he held his legs together. He unzipped, pulled four sweaters upward, finally he stood still long enough to urinate everywhere but in the toilet.

"Jesus Christ!" his aim was just a little off. He cleaned the mess that he made and sighed as he walked out the bathroom.

"Hmmm... Bradley must have left something for me." the brown paper bag was wrapped tightly with yellow rubber bands around it. No note. He sniffed it for bomb materials. He grabbed one of his shoes and stood halfway in the bathroom, aimed, and threw the shoe at it. "Nothing." he thought.

He scratched his ear, forehead, and stomach before approaching the bed. Before he picked the package up, he scratched again. He did this scratching thing every time he got nervous. Slowly, one rubber band at a time he removed them. After the fourth rubber band the sound of the paper bag begin to unravel. He peeked; looked, put his right hand in the bag that would change the rest of his life. It will cause him to lye, spy, and do what he never thought he would do in a life time. This would be the beginning of crossing the line of integrity. He had two chances to turn back. He didn't.

His bottom jaw dropped. What he held in his hand caused his fingers to tremble. He ran to the door and peeped through the peephole for fifty nine seconds.

"What the hell is going on?" he asked himself as he peeped through the peephole. He walked over to the bed and shoved it in the pillow case. He sweated heavily; he took off his layer of clothing. With just his light blue boxers on he tiptoed to the door again.

"Nobody!" he acted like a drug addict. He looked through the peephole for a hundred thirty two seconds. He felt like someone was watching him. He took his eye from the peephole, looked at his watch.

"Where is he? It's eighteen thirty five..." He saw Bradley walk up to his door. His heart pounded his chest like wild apes.

Bradley dropped his key, but he finally got into his room.

Na Min watched for awhile to make sure he was not followed, thinking the phone would ring in his hotel; he hoped he would call him soon.

He stood dumb founded with his back against the door. He curled his toes into the carpet. His palms itched and his arm pits perspired. He closed his eyes and waited.

"This has to be a joke, a test, but why?" he asked himself. He dug his nails into his palms trying to cure the itch. The knock at the door startled him. He peeped through the peephole. He opened the door and the room lit up from the hallway light.

Bradley entered the room with just the bathroom light on. "Na Min... well damn it's dark in here." He walked over to the dresser and flicked on the night stand light.

He stood there in his light blue boxers with the Winnie the Pooh printed on them. "So how was your day?" he asked with a little curiosity.

Bradley took a load off of his feet. "I talked to what's his name... and it's a go." he put out his cigarette in the ash tray. "I got everything lined up for Tuesday. The u-2 should be able to get some better photos to confirm this submarine facility." he said as he cleared his throat.

Na Min slid into his pants, right leg first. He hoped he would ask about the package on the bed. Maybe he had one on his bed that he was curious about.

Years later, he will wish he had asked about it.

"Well my end should be good to go. I dropped off the negs." Suddenly he yawned. "Boy, I am getting tired. What time in the morning?" Na Min asked him.

"It'll be a late start... go ahead and get some rest." Bradley stood up and headed towards the door.

"Hey just call me." Na Min said.

"Will do." the door closed behind him.

Five days later

Bradley and Na Min stood in the lobby of their hotel talking to a couple of Army officers.

"That gets me every time..." An officer said. They spoke about Vietnam. Their bodies were tipsy of liquor as they leaned on each other.

"So you boys are headed back to the DMZ in the morning?" Bradley asked them.

"Well unfortunately we are. Shit, to be honest, I can't wait to go back State side." He expressed with hands of a flying airplane landing on his palm. Their Rum had kicked in a while ago.

"Well..." looking at his watch, "...this old fart must head in." Na Min shook hands and said his good byes.

Later he entered his hotel room nervously. He quickly closed the door. He looked at the bed and felt like falling to the floor, another package on his bed.

"Damn, damn, damn..." he sighed. He used both of his hands to cover his face and slowly dragged them down his chin. He no longer looked through the peephole. His alcohol slowly reduced its affect. The party was over. Reality was smacking him in the face. This was the fourth package. He was pretty sure that the content is the same as before, fifteen thousand dollars American. It made him more nervous that he had not said anything. He opened it. He sighed. He felt like any moment there would be agents rushing into his room to arrest him, including Agent Bradley.

"Oh my God, what am I getting myself into" he looked up at the ceiling. He grabbed the package and threw it against the wall, knocking over a flower pot.

There was a note, and photos that lay on the floor among the money. He felt like throwing up. This is the classic case of black mail. He looked at the picture of him passing a newspaper to a known foreign national. It looked like he was doing nothing wrong. The next picture was of him counting a huge amount of money in the hotel room. He felt like he was trapped, cornered.

He read the note, "Hello... there is no way out. We have you counting your money, exchanging documents, which contained secrets. Meet me at the coffee shop across the street in the morning eight am."

He bald the note up into his palm, and gritted his teeth. His left eye lid twitched when his blood pressure rose, and it twitched none stop. He sighed deeply as he just let his body fall backwards on to the bed. He grabbed the bed spread with his hands and covered his face. He knew he had not betrayed his country, but he felt guilty, looked guilty, and if it got out that he is a trader. He would die without the honor of a true American hero.

To purchase the full book go to
nostalgicblood.com or any book store

For Nostalgic Blood apparel go to
nostalgicsociety.com

nostalgicsociety.com

Made in the USA
Columbia, SC
17 June 2021